THE HUNTER'S CURSE

THE HUNTER'S CURSE

JAMIE LEE FRY

BIGMOUNTAIN PUBLISHING

BOOK TWO OF
THE DARK MAGIC SERIES:

THE HUNTER'S CURSE

JAMIE LEE FRY

Print edition ISBN: 9798988215608
E-book edition ISBN: 9798988215615
Barnes & Noble Edition ISBN: 9781737120292

First edition: September 2023
10 9 8 7 6 5 4 3 2 1

WWW.AUTHORJAMIELEEFRY.COM

This is a work of fiction. Names, characters, places, and incidents either are the product of the author's imagination or are used fictitiously, and any resemblance to actual persons, living or dead, business establishments, events or locales is entirely coincidental.

FOR MY DAD, WITH LOVE

JAMIE LEE FRY

CHAPTER 01
IT'S BEEN A DAY

The only sound in the forest is the echo of Tahlia's weeping. Her high-pitched sobs clutch onto every ounce of the earth before bouncing down my eardrums. It stirs up a surge of energy inside me I can't explain.

I want to run to Tahlia—to help her. But I'm unsure what I should do. There is no protocol for this type of situation. She's in pain. Not a physical pain, but an emotional, aching kind of agony. She's confused, and I would be too if I were her.

Just as Callen promised, his parents are here cleaning up our mess. I don't know what we would have done if they hadn't arrived when they did. But the reality of the situation is hitting Tahlia hard. Their presence makes little sense to her. She doesn't know what they are—yet. And the fact that they aren't asking us questions doesn't help the matter at hand. It's only confusing her more.

"Callen, take everyone to our house now," Tahlia's mom commands, then turns her back to us as she consults with her husband.

Tahlia's dad is tending to Anna's lifeless, pale body; she's lying helplessly on the forest floor. It's still hard to believe what happened here less than an hour ago.

I can't help but stare as the man presses his hands on her open wound. He then releases the pressure and slowly lifts his arms above her body, letting them hover there momentarily. I study him as his lips move quickly, but I hear no words; he's careful and quiet. When he pauses, his eyes divert to the bloody, jagged gash down her chest. But something strange happens. The blood slowly recedes into the cut, with her skin sealing back together.

I peel my intrigued gaze away to see if anyone else noticed, but no one appears fazed. They didn't see what I did.

"Mom. Dad," Tahlia cries, pleading for their attention.

But neither of them responds to their distraught daughter's request.

Instead, her mother turns to me. "Give me your house keys," she demands.

I quickly produce the keyring, letting it dangle from my hand. She coldly snatches it from my grip. Her unfriendly demeanor sends shivers down my spine.

"Do you give me permission to enter your home?"

"Um, yes," I stutter.

The woman returns to her husband, bends over, and together they lift Anna's body, moving her away from the carnage of our circle. Their pace quickens as they retreat further into the dense thicket of towering, ominous trees. The sight of Anna's body being hauled away leaves me with a bone-chilling sensation that's escalating with Tahlia's unrelenting cries for answers.

"Why are they here, Callen? Please, tell me how our parents know what to do. Please. I'm so confused," she pleads, dropping to her knees and releasing another explosion of tortured emotions.

Her pain causes another ripple of unease in my stomach.

Callen's eyes flare with confliction. "Now's not the time, Tahlia. You'll get your answers soon. Please trust me."

Riley pulls me close; my skin burns where his flesh touches mine. But I don't care. I wiggle further into his embrace, finding temporary comfort in his arms. He kisses the top of my head, making my mouth involuntarily turn upward. I nuzzle my face into his shoulder, letting myself stay there with my eyes closed for a second. But when I emerge, my miniscule moment of peace is derailed.

Callen's watching us.

It's only a side eyed glare, but it's unmistakably in our direction. I stare back, letting him know he's busted. He shifts quickly on his feet, directing his attention back to his sister in need. He bends down, cradles his hands underneath the hollows of her arms, and gently tugs her upright. Tahlia fights him, twisting and kicking. The sound of her heel cracking into Callen's shin echoes painfully through the air. Callen's features tighten, but he doesn't flinch.

"How could you lie to me!" Tahlia screams. "My whole life is a lie. There's something you're not telling me! I know it."

"Not now, Tahlia. We need to go. You heard mom," Callen says, directing his sister toward our trail out of the forest.

Tahlia unsteadily crosses the lush field of green grass, meeting up with Jessa and Margo, who have been uncharacteristically quiet. Her sobbing doesn't cease, but at least she's in motion. Jessa, who's still recovering, takes Tahlia's hand, and my three friends walk in the direction of my house, away from this nightmare.

"What about my dad? Is it safe to leave him unattended?" Riley asks. "Maybe we should stay."

"He's unconscious. My parents will be right back. We need to go now," Callen responds.

"Hold on a second," I say, walking toward my enemy. I bend over and yank on the leather book sticking out of Tim's back pocket. My hand scratches along the ground as I tug it free. "I want my diary back," I hiss into his unconscious ear. Thankfully, Tim doesn't move.

I'm also not leaving without my spellbook and the knife that nearly killed me. I trust no one with these precious items, not even my friends. Well, maybe Margo, but that's it.

"Izzy, that's a murder weapon. Are you sure you should touch it?" Riley fearfully asks as I pick up the blood-stained knife. "Do you think maybe we should report this? I don't think we're thinking clearly."

A soft chuckle escapes from my belly. "It's not like we can call the police and report one of their own as a murderer and expect them to take us seriously. Your dad is a well-respected man in this community. Everyone knows and loves him. I'm the new kid in town with family rumors the length of the high school football field. Plus, what would we say? Your dad is a hunter, and he killed a witch. Oh, and

I'm in danger too because I'm also a witch, so you better lock him up. I'm taking the knife."

"Riley, bro, you need to trust my parents will handle things," Callen says.

"Let's get out of here," I direct the guys.

With my knife, diary, and book in tow, I follow Riley and Callen out of the forest. We sneak past my house, but my dad isn't home yet. I glance at my phone. It's almost five o'clock. He's late. But this works to our benefit.

The girls are waiting by Jessa's Jeep that's currently glamoured from Callen's spell. We haven't told Jessa the bad news yet—we have to destroy her Jeep. But that's a problem for another time. Right now, we need to get out of here before we ruin everything, and my dad sees us.

"I think it's best if we stick together," Callen suggests. "We can get the Jeep later."

Thankfully, Jessa's too tired to put up a fight. All six of us squeeze into Callen and Tahlia's mom's Wagoneer. I slide onto Riley's lap, alleviating the space issue. Everyone instantly falls quiet once Callen pulls onto the street. I have an elevated view of Tahlia in the front seat, rocking herself into a somber silence. A few tears fall from her chin, but she doesn't react. She simply continues to rock back and forth. Callen reaches over and grabs his sister's hand. He squeezes it tightly. That's sweet, especially for how much I've observed them fighting today.

I lean back, letting my head rest on Riley's shoulder, hoping my assumed boyfriend—the witch-hunter-in-waiting won't snap and kill me right here in the car. I'm trapped and there is nowhere to flee.

Luckily, I make it to Tahlia's house unscathed.

Once inside Tahlia and Callen's large estate, everyone scatters. Jessa jets to the couch for a much-needed nap. She's still recovering, so I don't press her to stay with us. Tahlia dashes up the grand staircase, and the sound of a door slamming makes me think she's going to need a minute alone.

"Make yourselves at home," Callen says, then disappears up the stairs after his sister.

"Follow me." Margo gestures, directing us into the kitchen.

Riley takes a seat on one of the several high barstools along the black granite kitchen island. Margo opens the refrigerator, pulls some items from the shelves, and places them on the counter.

I saunter over to the sink with my knife. I let the hot water flush down the blade, ridding it of Anna's blood and Tim's fingerprints. The reddish water turns clear as it swirls down the drain. I stand by my earlier thoughts of keeping this situation close to those who need to know. After all, we're dealing with magic and things outside of normal comprehension. It's what I need to do to keep myself safe. No hunter will attempt to kill me with my own blood again. Lesson learned—always clean our blade after each session.

I reach for a handful of paper towels because I can't help but think it would be rude to use their fancy kitchen towel on a murder weapon.

As I dry my knife, I scan the room for a safe place to store my items. My eyes land on a row of hooks in the mudroom just off the kitchen. I recognize Tahlia's leather messenger school bag hanging amongst several other backpacks. She won't miss it. She has plenty to choose from.

I grab it. It's empty. Perfect.

I haul the bag to the kitchen island and carefully slide each of my items inside. I don't know how today will proceed, and I'll feel better knowing my stuff is concealed on me. As I sling the bag over my shoulder, my stomach grumbles, reminding me I haven't eaten all day.

"Come sit," Margo says, patting the barstool beside Riley.

She places a plate in front of me. "It's a turkey sandwich on a hoagie bun with lettuce, cheese, and mayo." Margo smiles, sliding a second plate in front of Riley.

I shouldn't eat at a time like this, but my tummy groans, so I don't argue.

Riley lifts the top of his bun and studies the contents of his sandwich. I don't peg him as a picky eater, and he hasn't said a word since we arrived, so I know he's processing the day's events.

I take a huge bite, and the flavors hit my tastebuds in all the right places. "Do you think they have some salty chips to go with it?" I greedily ask, wanting to satisfy my stomach now that I've started.

Margo tosses me a bag of sea salt and vinegar chips. I place a handful on my plate and pass the bag to Riley, but he doesn't reach for it. He's replaced his bun top, but now he's staring off into space, locked away in his thoughts.

I think the rush of what happened in the forest is wearing off. He was my hero today. Riley saved me from his dad, but now the reality of it all is settling in. We were all in panic mode, just going with the flow, and well, now it's different. It's understandable he's acting this way.

Being from a family of hunters and watching your dad kill someone can't be easy.

I should feel sadder, but somehow, I have comfort knowing Anna is still with me. I'm sure when I'm alone, everything will hit me all at once, but I'm doing well for the time being.

There are a lot of unknowns and questions that need to be answered. Surprisingly, Margo and Riley aren't asking them right now.

I shove the last bite of my sandwich into my mouth as a door slams upstairs. Margo and I share a concerned glance.

I wonder if we should check on Tahlia.

"She's going to need some time with this," Callen says, rounding the corner into the kitchen, answering my thoughts.

"It's been a day," I respond.

Callen locks on my gaze. "I told her." His words come out quiet, meant for my ears only, but the way Margo and Riley lean in, I know they heard.

"Oh," I say, shocked. "Like everything?"

Margo's eyes widen, and Riley's mouth parts open with a shallow hum of a question sputtering under his breath. His inaudible sentence pauses, causing me to twist my head in curiosity.

Tahlia's mom is standing in the doorway, watching us with an impassive expression resting across her face.

"Follow me now," she says.

Callen, Margo, Riley, and I do as we're asked, waking Jessa on the way through the living room. The five of us follow Callen's parents down a long hallway, passing several closed doors before entering the last one on the left. It's a spacious office with a wide oak desk facing a window. Plaques and framed certificates line the opposite wall, leaving one wall completely barren.

Each of my friend's eyes marvel with curiosity.

No one asks the question we're all thinking; what on earth are we doing in this room? My words are failing me, and I'm OK with that. The less attention, the better right now, especially in the presence of a hunter.

Callen's dad stoically turns toward the vacant wall. Without explanation, he presses his hand against the left side about halfway down.

A murmur of confusion and curiosity pounds through my stomach, making my insides churn in anticipation.

The partition slowly glides open, revealing a staircase.

Not what I was expecting at all.

Who are these people?

Without looking back, he enters through the doorway. His wife stays behind, gesturing for us to follow him.

I'm not sure this is a good idea, but once again, my words are stalled in my throat. My feet obey the motion of the crowd, ignoring my gut feeling to run and never look back.

My friends and I heedfully file down a narrow staircase faintly illuminated by light fixtures resembling Victorian oil lamps.

Creepy.

Just as my newfound claustrophobia sets in, the hallway darkens. I shift my gaze over my shoulder to see the door gliding shut behind Callen's mom.

I choke down a choppy breath, trying to push down the fear overtaking my body.

Everyone ahead of me comes to an abrupt halt, nearly rocking me off balance. We wait as Callen's dad presses numbers into a touchpad lock. He checks over his shoulder several times, ensuring we aren't watching him. In unison, we all direct our gaze downward.

Then, one by one, we walk through a thick-framed doorway. Immediately, I know this isn't an average basement. The thickness of the walls, the heavy door, and the large object at the end of the walkway seals my assumptions—a cage.

CHAPTER 02
YOU SHOULD BE DEAD

They have a cage.

An actual cage. With restraints. In their home. An entire enclosure, just chilling in their secret basement.

Normal people stuff, right?

This must be a dream.

Seriously, stuff like this doesn't happen in the real world.

Yup, just a dream. No, more like a vivid nightmare.

The absurdity of my entire day is making me question everything now. None of it seems like it really happened.

Because if it did, then Anna is dead. Tim killed her and almost sliced me with the same knife coated in witches' blood. My witchy friends and I brought Jessa back from the edge of death. Oh, and my dream guy, who finally kissed me—I wouldn't mind keeping that part—but the part about him being a witch hunter can vaporize into the abyss when I wake up from this horrific nightmare.

It's almost comical because it's so crazy. I want to laugh, but my body has other plans. I squeeze my eyes tight until a stream of tears slips past my eyelids, racing down my cheeks. I open my eyes, and it's still there—the cage.

Nope, not a nightmare. Today really happened. I can't help but wonder why I felt so calm and so in control earlier. But now, being here in this basement, I'm losing it—quickly.

Plus, everyone is staring at me.

Am I supposed to say something?

Why do I suddenly feel like this is all landing on my shoulders?

Will someone please say something? I can't take the silence any longer.

But no one speaks. No one hears my internal cry for help, not even Callen. I choke down the chunks of fear layering in my throat, keeping me from voicing my concerns. I swallow hard to suffocate the feeling, so it doesn't rise again and catch me off guard. I need to be confident. I must not show any signs of weakness. I pat my face dry with the palms of my hands before addressing the darkly lit room.

I can do this.

"Hi, I'm Izzy. I'm a bloodline witch," I say the words like I'm introducing myself to a support group. "My Gran-gran is the reason this whole thing started, I think."

I shakily extend my hand toward Tahlia's dad, but he doesn't move. Instead, he stares icily at me with velvety eyes that match his son's. I slowly let my arm fall to my side, but his gaze doesn't drop.

"So, you're the Beswick girl," Tahlia's mom says. Her flat and calm words make it hard to gauge her statement's intent.

I take a deep breath, remembering what Callen said about his mom. She's a hunter. But her son and husband, who's still creepily staring at me, are my kind—witches. So, how this whole thing works, I don't have a clue. But I'm not family. I'm a bloodline witch. An outsider. An intruder. My presence has set things in motion that are out of my control. They cleaned up our mess, so they know a lot—I trusted them—was that wrong?

"Yes, I am," I finally respond, gaping past her. My eyes land on the thick metal poles that make up the homemade jail cell that, for some reason, the Latham-Hart family conveniently has in their basement.

Is the cage for me?

"Izzy, do you understand the danger you put everyone in?" Tahlia's mom asks. Her hands rest on her hips while she angrily taps her foot in a persistent rhythm.

She's intimidating.

Perhaps it's the fact that she's towering over me. The woman has a good five or six inches on me. She's even an inch taller than her husband. Or it could be her robust biceps that are well-defined under her tight, black, long-sleeved shirt. But it's probably her beauty. It's just what I expected, with her creamy, ivory, flawless skin and her bouncy, unruly auburn curls that extend outward, creating a sphere around her head. She's gorgeous, except for the little vein jutting out from her forehead that's currently pulsating, waiting for an answer.

She wants a simple response, but I don't have one. Instead, I stare doe-eyed at her, hoping for forgiveness and kindness. After all, I almost died in the forest too. Throw a girl a bone here. Or should I say broom? Yes, throw a girl a broom here. My lip curls at my cleverness, but I quickly catch myself and bite at my bottom lip to keep it from bending upward any further.

This isn't a joke.

Anna's dead.

I watched her die.

But I don't know how to react or respond, and my attempt at humoring myself is my mind's only coping mechanism at this moment.

Get a hold of yourself, Izzy.

I nervously tuck my straggler hair behind my ears and clear my throat several times before landing on my generic response. "It's not like I wanted this to happen," I say the words under my breath, dropping my head down so far that my neck cracks.

Do they not see the stress I'm currently under? Of course, I didn't want this to happen. I wanted to be normal and get through my senior year without any attention.

So much for that.

Why aren't my friends under interrogation? Why aren't they being probed with questions too? And hell, when was I nominated speaker of the group?

"What do you expect me to say?" My words roll off my lips before my brain can even process them.

Tahlia's mom clenches her jaw tightly, holding her glare in my direction, keeping me on pins and needles. "Please excuse us for a moment," she says, pulling her husband away into the corner next to the cage.

I bet they're discussing whether to shove me inside of it

right now. *Keep the novice witch girl locked up until they can figure out how to deal with her.* Although, I can't confirm that's what they're discussing, and not for lack of trying, either.

I direct my attention behind me. Riley, Jessa, and Margo have their backs pressed tightly against the red brick wall. Each of them with the same expression: confusion mixed with sadness. It's no wonder they haven't spoken up. They're frightened too. Callen has yet to speak one word, making me question his relationship with his parents. And Tahlia, she's MIA and has been since the moment we arrived. She should be here with us. She's bold. She'd be asking questions.

"Izzy," Tahlia's mom calls out, pulling me away from my thoughts. "I'm going to need you to start from the beginning and tell me everything that happened. We"—she nods to her husband—"need to hear the entire story. Callen gave us the CliffsNotes version when he called for help. And as you can imagine, there are some plot holes to fill in."

"OK," I respond, gawking at the intriguing couple, wondering how the heck their relationship is possible.

But I'm quickly sidetracked by Tahlia's dad, who is eerily replicating the same stillness that first creeped me out about his daughter in the cafeteria. I guess I know where she got that trait from. It's quickly becoming her dad's most prominent attribute, making me very uncomfortable.

I swallow hard, allowing myself a moment before unleashing my story. "Mrs. Latham-Hart—"

She cuts me off, "Just call me Bree. It's a mouthful to say my hyphenated name. Oh, and my husband, you can just call him Barrett." She shows a hint of a smile.

There almost seems to be tenderness in her words, and I latch onto them, wanting her to like and approve of me, so she doesn't—well, kill me—that whole hunter thing.

"OK, thank you, Mrs. Lat—I mean Bree. I moved here a few months ago with my dad. My Gran-gran died five years ago, and we inherited her house. I-s-o-b-e-l Beswick," I say her name slowly, waiting for a reaction. She already knows I'm the Beswick girl, but there's always a reaction when I say her name. But Bree doesn't react.

"Strange things started happening when I moved in, and the girls told me of rumors—Isobel being a witch. I thought they were crazy, but they wanted to see her house."

"And you just let some strangers in your home, snooping around things that don't belong to you," Bree hisses.

There goes the kindness.

"Yes, I guess if you put it like that. But they do belong to me. I inherited the home and all the belongings inside," I respond.

Bree lets a frustrated grin pull her features downward as she breathes heavily through her nose.

"Long story short. We found a book of spells, proving that Gran-gran was indeed a witch, and the rumors were true, even the one about my love life being cursed," I respond.

I assume they know about the curse, because hell, everyone in this town knows things.

Riley glides closer, tucking himself behind me. I can't see him, but I know he's there.

"And you thought you could take magic into your own hands?" Bree lectures.

"We all thought we could," I respond.

"And how does Officer Tim play into things?" Bree asks.

"My dad and Tim are friends. He's been helping my dad repair our house."

"He was snooping," Riley says, grabbing my hand behind my back. It burns.

"Yes, snooping, gathering information on us," I add.

Tahlia's dad shifts on his feet, reminding me he's not a statue. Sweat dots his golden-brown forehead. His skin glistens each time he moves. He reminds me a lot of Callen, except without the curls, and Barrett has much broader shoulders.

"Does he have anything important on him right now?" Barrett asks.

"I don't think so," I slowly respond, keeping the part about the diary he attempted to steal twice to myself.

Barrett yanks an old-school walkie-talkie from his back pocket. "Search him," he says into the speaker.

Who is he talking to?

"Where is my dad? Is he here? What did you do with him?" Riley questions, pressing himself into me, squeezing my hand tight.

"He's being processed," Bree responds.

"By whom?" Riley asks. His leg restlessly taps against mine.

Riley is worried. I get it. I'd be worried too. Even considering that his dad is a murderer. It's not like he can just turn off his love for his father in one quick swoop.

"That's none of your concern," Barrett says.

"But he's my dad. I have the right to know," Riley insists.

"Riley, you will see him soon," Barrett responds, walking

to the far end of the dungeon-like basement, pressing the walkie to his ear.

"So, Anna Beswick?" Bree coaxes my attention. "She left town a long time ago. I didn't think we'd see her face again around here. What brought her back?"

"Anna—my grandma—sensed I was doing magic, and she came to stop me, but she was too late. We had already done a spell, and apparently, it went awry."

I don't elaborate because I'm unsure how much I should tell them. I'm leaving out the parts about Jessa hitting Megan, Jessa's Jeep, and the black chunks. The fewer people who know about all that, the better.

"Anna stayed behind to clean up our mess, and that's when Tim found her, I guess. He held her hostage or something, then killed her in front of us. And then he tried to kill me."

Again, I'm leaving out a lot of details.

"What did you do with Anna?" I question.

"We took care of her," Bree responds, avoiding eye contact.

"What does that mean?" A lump lodges in my throat, so I swallow hard, choking it down, but it keeps working its way back up.

Bree takes a deep breath, pulling her wild hair away from her face, gathering it behind her head, and tying it back with a hairband. "We made it look like she came for a surprise visit, leaving her luggage in your foyer for your father to find when he returns home. We're lucky he didn't show up and catch us. I left her nice shoes she was wearing at the back door and placed her boots on her, making it appear she went out for a walk, since no one was home."

Bree locks her eyes on mine. "Izzy, we had to make it look like an accident. Anna Beswick slipped and fell off a cliff above the stream a quarter mile from your circle, about a mile from your house. Hikers will probably find her body sooner than later."

"Oh." I gasp at the irony.

Anna pushed Sondra off a cliff, and that's what Bree and Barrett did to her. I know she was already dead, but that's not how I assumed they'd *handle* things.

"It was the easiest solution," Bree responds, tossing my keys at me. "We can't have the authorities snooping around our business, especially when we're already dealing with one of their own. This needs to be a cut-and-dried case— an accident."

"What about her wound? Tim stabbed her with a knife. Won't they suspect foul play when she's found?" I know the answer, but I'm curious to see if Barrett admits to healing Anna's wound in front of everyone.

"Magic," Barrett responds, waggling his fingers toward me.

OK, so not a secret.

A rapping on the thick door startles me, sending my mind into a frenzy, wondering who else is here.

My breath catches in my throat.

"You can enter," Barrett says into his walkie.

The click of the lock releasing makes my heart drop into my stomach, making me regret the turkey sandwich I recently ate that's slowly moving up my esophagus. I swallow hard as the heavy door swings wide open, slamming into the brick wall behind it. My hand burns hot as a pair of men stagger into the room, one trying to control the other.

I take a step back, nestling myself between Riley and Jessa.

A tall, burly, bouncer-like man shoves a bloody-faced prisoner in a black jumpsuit up against the thick poles of the jail cell. The prisoner twists his head, letting his eyes find mine. Even through the ill lighting and all the blood, I know those eyes. Those haunting eyes belong to Officer Tim Hawkins.

Tim struggles within the man's grip, twisting and kicking. "You should be dead, witch," he hisses.

"Lock him up," Barrett orders the man.

CHAPTER 03
ALL LIES

Tim's words pierce through me, and my skin crawls with fire. A tainted mixture of emotions twists through my abdomen: sadness, sickness, resentment, and betrayal. I never wanted to hate this man, but now, I have no choice. He killed Anna. Tim and I will forever, from that moment, be mortal enemies. Sure, his words sting, but at least I'm alive. I'm here to fight another day.

I almost want to laugh, thinking about how good of an actor Tim is, pretending to care about my dad and me. I never imagined he was a hunter. Yet, for some reason, it pains me to see him like this.

I don't want to feel any sympathy for him. I can't show any weakness. I must be strong.

Riley.

My heart breaks for him. That must be it. I'm sad for Riley seeing his dad like this.

Riley.

Or is my heart breaking for me? What if he turns into his dad? What if we're being naïve, thinking we have a chance?

Our days are numbered. Five of them, to be exact. I'm lucky he hasn't shown signs of hatred toward me—yet. Sondra shifted sooner than she should've, but she was a bitch deep down, so maybe it manifested quicker because of that.

My chest tightens at the thought.

"Oh, come on, Bree, it doesn't have to be like this," Tim begs, switching his tone, drawing me back to the bloody man in a black jumpsuit that used to be my family's friend.

"I'm sorry, Tim. Your behavior was erratic, and you put my children in danger. This is where you belong right now," Bree says.

"Traitor," Tim yells.

The bouncer-like man directs Tim into the cage, shoving him into the far corner, letting his body slam against the thick metal poles for a second time.

Tim moans in pain.

I feel sick watching this. Couldn't they have left us upstairs for this part? Riley shouldn't see this. None of us need to see this.

I refuse to let the tear that's threatening to spill over touch my skin. I take a deep breath, hoping to dry it up, but it doesn't.

It's on the verge of dropping.

I can't blink, or it will fall.

Tim doesn't deserve my tears. But Riley does. So, I let this one release. For Riley. For Us. Not Tim. I keep my eyes pinned on the cage. The door is open. I won't feel safe until it's locked. Visions of Tim standing above me, ready to slice me open, cause me to tense up.

"Witch lover," Tim shouts, spitting in the man's eye.

The man doesn't flinch or even wipe it away. He remains professional and calm as he backs out of the cage, leaving Tim a prisoner inside. The 'witch lover' locks the door with a long silver key hanging amongst several similar keys on a keyring. I sure hope this is their only cage, and right now, I'm grateful I'm not the one inside of it. With that thought, a sigh of relief escapes me.

"What are you going to do with him?" Riley asks, threading his fingers between mine.

"I'm not sure yet, but we can't have him on the streets. We can't trust him, but I can't kill him. It's part of our treaty," Bree responds.

"Treaty?" I question.

Riley lets his fingers slip from mine, taking a shy step forward. "I want to know more about this treaty, but first, I need to know your role in all of this. Are you both witches?"

Riley, Jessa, and Margo have no idea what they're about to hear. I only found out hours ago, but it's been nice understanding what I'm dealing with. They must be so terrified and confused.

Jessa fidgets next to me, eager to piggyback on Riley's question. It's what Jessa does. "Yeah, and is someone going to tell us why my best friend's parents have a jail cell in their basement? Who the hell are you people?"

Margo nods, agreeing to Jessa's question.

"Yes, Mom and Dad, are you going to enlighten us?" Tahlia's snooty voice echoes from the top of the stairwell. Her mood seems to have spiked from earlier.

Barrett lunges forward with his eyes pinning on the doorway. "You didn't make sure the top door latched?" he questions his bouncer.

"Sorry, boss. My hands were busy," the man says, nodding to Tim in the cage. "It won't happen again."

"Better not," Barrett says sternly.

Tahlia lets her hand glide down the railing as she slowly makes her way down the steps and through the second door that's still wide open. "What the hell is this place? I had no clue this room existed. Someone better start explaining, or I'm going to freak out!"

Bree extends her arms outward as her daughter glides by, but Tahlia sidesteps her mother's welcoming embrace. Instead, she chooses us. Jessa loops her arm through Tahlia's, tugging her close, pulling her into our impenetrable friendship barrier along the cold red brick wall, like it's us against them.

"So?" Tahlia demands.

"Sweetie, you were never meant to find out about any of this," Bree says.

"That's bullshit!" Tahlia screams. "Callen told me what you are. What we are."

"T, what are you talking about?" Jessa asks with confusion resting heavily on her face, leaving a crease on her forehead.

"Oh, you don't know. Because apparently, everyone knew but me. I'm a half-breed, just like Anna said. My parents are liars. My mom is a hunter, and my dad is a witch. A witch, like everyone thought Isobel was. I'm a freak, just like Izzy. No, wait. I'm worse because I'm a freaking mutt. A half-breed witch, hunter-hybrid that has no place in this world."

Freak just like Izzy. Her words sting a little, but I know she's just lashing out.

"And Callen?" Margo questions, slowly stepping away from Tahlia's brother.

Even though Margo and I aren't touching, I can sense her fear, but she doesn't have anything to worry about with Callen. He's on our side. He's one of us.

Barrett clears his throat, taking a gentle step toward us. My body tenses, even though I know what he's about to say.

"My son is a witch. Yes, it's true we're an anomaly. We shouldn't exist as we do, but love is more powerful sometimes. Bree and I had children; some would say that was wrong, but we don't agree. We make it work. My sweet baby girl, you'll find your truth on your eighteenth birthday, just like your brother did. Right now, you're a hunter and a witch, both sides lying dormant, but both bloodlines course through your veins fighting for power. You're special, Tahlia, and soon, one side will take over. We won't know until it happens."

"Like I said, I'm the freak." Tahlia whimpers. "How is that special?"

Barrett's head drops. I'm sure this isn't how they wanted Tahlia to find out this information. It's a delicate subject. I bet Callen had a gentler conversation and without an audience.

Poor Tahlia.

"I hate to ask this, but I can't help but wonder how this all works—you being a hunter and, well, them being witches? Don't you have the desire to kill them?" I ask.

Tim huffs to himself inside his cage. "Yeah, Bree. Tell the kids how your relationship works. I'm sure my son and that witch will want to hear the lengths you go to."

Bree doesn't acknowledge Tim. Instead, she keeps her eyes fiercely pinned on Riley and me. "Don't get any ideas that this is easy. It's not. Hence the cage. Sometimes, the desire to hunt them is there, and I need some time away until the urges subside. I've been doing this a long time, and I've learned to control my impulses… mostly."

"Your work trips?" Tahlia questions.

"Yes, dear. I never went on those so-called trips. I was down here in that cage. Sid"—she nods to the bouncer—"he would take care of me."

"Is—is he a hunter too?" I stutter, wondering how much I should let my guard down around these people. I'm already being too carefree around Riley and Bree.

"No, Sid isn't one of us. But he's special," Bree states.

The word *special* sits like fire on my tongue, but I don't ask why. I have more important questions that need answers first.

"Why didn't Tim turn on us sooner?" I ask.

Tim chuckles. "We're calculated beings. We act when the time is right."

"Tim is correct. The urges—they're always there. You learn to master them over time and act when it's best to keep from being detected by society. New hunters don't have that control. So, Riley, you need to be careful. But even old hunters can slip," Bree responds.

Riley's body goes limp against mine.

"What the actual fuck?" Jessa shrieks.

"Language, Jessa," Bree hisses.

"So, this treaty?" I encourage Bree to continue, ignoring Jessa's outburst and cry for attention.

"I'm sorry, dear, but it doesn't include your family. The Beswicks went rogue a long time ago, but it protects my family and Margo's family," Bree says.

"What about mine?" Jessa asks.

"You don't need protection, Jessa. You're not like us," Bree says.

"Oh," Jessa responds.

Jessa's disappointment is evident as the weight of her shoulders drops against my arm. Typical Jessa. She should feel blessed no one wants to kill her. Just look at Tahlia. She had fun with the little bit of spellwork we did, but she knew the heaviness of it rested on me. But now things are different. Tahlia is different. And Jessa's jealous of that. Go figure.

"So, this treaty was drawn up to include the Latham-Harts, Hawleys, and Hawkins families," Bree begins.

"So, Margo's really a witch too?" Jessa asks, cutting Bree off.

"Margo comes from a complicated line of witches. But I suspect you already started to understand that?" Barrett says, responding for his wife.

Margo nods, nervously gripping her pendant necklace for comfort.

"This is a very complex mess, but I suppose before we tell you more about the treaty, we need to disclose everything we know. It's time. You're all involved more than you ever should have been. If Izzy hadn't shown up, none of this would have come to light the way it did," Barrett responds. "We've kept things under control in East Gate until recently."

I frown at the thought that all of this is my fault. But if the girls didn't push to see my house, none of this would have happened. I don't toss my friends under the bus. I remain quiet.

"Here come the lies," Tim hisses from his cage.

I shoot him an evil glare.

"Ignore him," Barrett says.

"Can't we continue this conversation upstairs?" I ask.

"It's safer down here," Barrett responds.

"How?" I demand.

"It's proofed for our safety; that's all you need to know," he responds.

Not an answer, but whatever.

"Anyway, this is our truth as it was passed down to us," Barrett says, glaring back at Tim. "So, back in the late sixteen hundreds, witchcraft hysteria was at its peak in Salem, Massachusetts, and with good reason. Witches were real, but the history books are missing the whole truth.

"Witches have always been around, hiding in the shadows, hoping to stay hidden from the world. Most practiced light magic: doing good for others like healing or assisting with food shortages by playing with weather patterns to ensure good crops. Of course, those good deeds went unnoticed, and that's good. They never wanted recognition.

"But when a witch practices dark magic, people notice. Most witches start out light and turn dark by craving more power. When a witch uses dark magic for greed, harm, or worse, they're usually being showy and drawing attention to themselves. That was the case with Isobel. See, life was different back then. Women didn't have rights, and men weren't expected to be kind to their wives. Yes, most were, but for those who weren't, society turned a blind eye. It wasn't their business.

"When Isobel's new husband died in a horrific way, the village suspected her of witchcraft. It didn't help that children were going into fits and getting sick. It only stirred the fire, so to speak. It had to be witchcraft—or so the villagers assumed, because it was the only thing that made sense at the time.

"Every day, more and more people were accused of witchcraft, whether they practiced or not. It didn't matter. It was easy to declare someone a witch. But the most powerful witches in Salem at the time were our ancestors. Margo's ancestor Lydia Bishop, my ancestor Dinah Abbott, Isobel Williams, formally Beswick, along with the rumored original witch of Salem, Elizabeth Crowley—the people in town knew her as the lady of potions."

I gasp, but quickly cover my blunder with a cough.

The lady of potions.

Isobel referenced the lady of potions in her diary. She said she was like her. It's more important than ever that I see the rest of the entries. I stroke the bag that hangs alongside my body.

Barrett continues with his story, which sounds pretty accurate so far. "They were practicing witches, so the townsfolk were correct in their accusations. But did that mean they should be tried and killed for it?" He shrugs his shoulders. "Anyway, The Wives of Salem Coven, as they were known to themselves, were rounded up. Dinah, Elizabeth, and Lydia were accused of crimes so minor it wasn't even worth recording, but they accused Isobel of murdering her husband by witchcraft. People said they saw him walk off the roof of his barn. The court says Isobel compelled him to kill himself."

Sounds about right. Add another dead husband to her list. It also appears she didn't keep his name either.

"Why wasn't any of this in the history books?" Riley asks.

"A lot of history never got recorded. These stories stayed alive by the ones who passed it down."

"Don't believe them, son. I told you—all lies," Tim says, seething from his jail cell. "They were witches who deserved a good hanging. So, does it matter what they did or didn't do?" His bottom lip curled upward in disgust.

"Believe what you want, but I must continue. You all need to understand this story if we're going to survive and go undetected from this point on." Barrett pauses, going still for a moment, then continuing with minimal animation.

"All four witches were set to stand trial. Elizabeth was first. While she was away being tested as a witch, the others were conspiring to escape. I believe in my heart they wanted to wait for their coven member, but something must have happened to put their plan into motion sooner."

"Lies," Tim interjects again. "A witch will betray her kind if that means her own security."

Barrett ignores Tim's words. I suppose they don't merit a response from a witch. He's taking the high ground.

Good for you, Barrett. Don't take his shit.

"Later, when Elizabeth returned to her cell to await her sentencing, her coven was gone—vanished. The other three witches escaped, presumably by one of their cloaking spells."

"See I told you," Tim says with a know-it-all tone. "Their own security came first."

Barrett subtly rolls his eyes. "Now, of course, spells are stronger with four, but these witches were natural, experienced witches who knew how to pull from the elements without being near them, and it worked. Well, kind of.

"Imagine how ticked Elizabeth was to be abandoned by her coven. Perhaps she tried to join them but couldn't. So, in her mind she chose the next best thing—revenge."

CHAPTER 04
TIMES THREE

"Revenge?" Tahlia questions, the words rolling off her tongue in a quivering whisper.

Barret nods. "I hate to be the one to admit this, but maybe Tim is right about *some* witches. Elizabeth chose revenge, and the bitterness of her decision filled her with a sense of hatred. She left a trail of tears and destruction for centuries to come." Barrett pulls in a quick breath. "Elizabeth trapped the three escaped witches between worlds. They were cloaked by their own spell, but damned there by Elizabeth's resentment."

"Wow, that's dark," Jessa says.

"It gets worse," Barret responds. "So, as Elizabeth sat with her anger, awaiting her sentencing, she conjured a secondary punishment. Unsure of the length of time they'd be trapped between worlds and wanting her coven to suffer forever, she placed a cur—"

Cutting him off, I sputter, "The bloodline curse." The words leave a metallic taste on my lips.

"Yes. That's Elizabeth's doing. Never mess with a scorned

witch. She wanted to ensure they paid for their betrayal."

"Wait, so you're telling us that you, Tahlia, Callen, and Margo are bloodline witches too?" Jessa questions, with jealousy layered in each name that rolls off her tongue.

"Pretty much." Barrett nods to his daughter, who's technically not a full witch—yet.

Tahlia's ancestor's blood courses through her veins, which, in hindsight, is what made our spell work. We got lucky. We've been so naïve and careless.

Barrett continues, "Elizabeth never wanted them to find happiness or love. Eventually, the first spell wore off. Dinah, Lydia, and Isobel were free to leave their purgatory in 1788. Dinah and Lydia relocated to East Gate. It was a new community and the perfect place to rebuild. They each had husbands for a short time. Of course, they died, but they had babies, who then carried on the curse. And so on, and so on. Over time, the magic diluted and was never practiced, but stories of their misfortune floated through the generations."

"What about Isobel?" I ask.

"She waited in her purgatory," he responds.

"For what reason?"

"Your guess is as good as mine. But I assume she was keeping her bloodline pure, waiting for the right time to emerge. As the story goes, she eventually left sometime in the nineteen hundreds and ended up in East Gate too. We assume she kept an eye on Lydia and Dinah. Of course, by the time she returned, they were long gone. So, she monitored their bloodlines. But none of their offspring showed any signs of magic. At least, that's what she thought, until recently."

"This is where the story gets interesting," Tim shouts from his cell. "Tell them how the hunters came to be, Bree. Tell the kids about our family's history. This one's a real doozy."

"Mom, what's he talking about?" Tahlia asks.

Bree clears her throat and sighs. "Well, Elizabeth wasn't satisfied with her first two curses and had a lot of time on her hands awaiting her death. So, to ensure there would be absolutely no chance of their survival, she did the unthinkable. Elizabeth summoned two guards to her cell: Talbot Hawkins and Timothy Latham.

"She cast an intricate spell on them—more like cursed them. These men were compelled to forever hunt and extricate all witches. To seal the curse, Elizabeth knew the first blood of a witch had to be shed. She made the greatest sacrifice: herself.

"Timothy and Talbot killed their first witch that night, locking in the hunter's curse—bonding their bloodlines to it forever."

"So, a witch did this to her own kind?" Margo asks.

"Sounds crazy, but it's true," Barrett responds.

"If she could do all of that, then I'm sure she could have escaped," I respond.

"I wish I had an answer to that. Perhaps she enjoyed the torture—the dark magic. I really don't know," Barret says. "Maybe she's still out there somewhere pulling the strings." He uncomfortably laughs.

Tim bangs on the metal poles of his cage. "And the math

is simple. There are more hunters than witches. We're good at disguising ourselves until it's time to kill. Eventually, we will fulfill our mission."

A fury of annoyance vibrates under my skin. "Can't you just stop hunting?"

Tim groans. "It's not that simple. It's what we were bred to do."

He sounds brainwashed.

"I hate to say this, but Tim is right. He and I are fifteenth-generation hunters, making Riley a sixteenth-generation hunter and possibly Tahlia. There are a lot of us out there. So many, we've lost count," Bree says.

Sondra. But at least that's one less hunter in the world. Oh my God. What am I thinking? This is ridiculous. No one should die because of what they're born into.

"Can't you all agree to disagree? Sounds like you're all supernatural beings that didn't choose this path," Jessa quips. "Hello, it's 2022, not 1692. Can't you just stop this and live like normal people?"

"One would think, but it doesn't work that way," Bree responds.

"Well, it seems you two figured it out—how to co-exist," Riley adds.

"Barrett and I fell in love before we understood what we were and how severe the consequences of our love could be. My parents forbid us to date, but we were madly in love, and nothing was going to stop us from being together. I had no clue I was a hunter, and Barrett had only recently started having things happen that he couldn't explain."

"I swore I could change the outcome of certain events with my thoughts. I thought I was going crazy because every time I focused on something, it would happen," Barrett responds.

"His magic was blooming, and it was hard for me to ignore. And I didn't understand what was happening inside of me. A switch flipped, and on my eighteenth birthday, I nearly killed him. That was the first time Barrett truly experienced his magic. It was there all along, playing a tiny role in his life until that night when he saved himself from me."

"Barrett's dad and my parents kept our heritage a secret until that night. I'm not even sure they believed it themselves, but the proof was hard to argue against. My parents didn't hunt. But they did things in their past that would suggest otherwise. We never talked about it. And I don't think Barrett's father wanted to accept that the stories were true. That meant he lost his love to a stupid curse. It seemed so ridiculous until it wasn't."

"Why hasn't the curse killed you?" I respond. I quickly realize how harsh my words sound, but it's too late to reel them back in.

Bree draws in a long, thoughtful breath. "I suppose it could have at some point, but after a while, it didn't happen. We assumed our curse was loving a different supernatural being, not of the same cloth. I'm sure Elizabeth didn't factor in this kind of love—one of her hunters falling for a cursed witch." Bree laughs. "The curse could have killed me, or I could have killed him. Either way, I'm grateful for the time I've spent with Barrett and my children. I wouldn't change it.

"And… I don't think Elizabeth accounted for the four of you existing. I mean, she tried—times three—to ensure the end of your bloodlines, but she failed. Callen, Izzy, Margo, and Tahlia, you're the four most powerful witches since 1692. You did the unimaginable—you broke the bloodline curse. Now we don't need to worry."

Things start clicking in my brain. One piece after another, falling into place.

My body boils with rage like a kettle that's about to blow. I shake my hand free from Riley and lunge toward Barrett.

"You knew about the curse since you were eighteen. There were enough bloodline witches in this town"—I drop to my knees, releasing loud sobs—"you could have saved her. You could have saved my mom."

CHAPTER 05
THE TREATY

My body shakes with emotions as I sob uncontrollably in the middle of the basement. If they had done something sooner, she'd be alive. That thought cuts through me, leaving me open and exposed.

My mom. I miss her.

"Izzy, I wish it were that simple. I'm so sorry your mother's gone. I wish I could have prevented her death. I was aware of the curse, but I didn't know how to undo it. You have to believe that." Barrett pauses. "But somehow, you kids figured it out."

I stroke the messenger bag with my book inside of it.

Forces called to us—showing us the way.

We broke the curse by accident. We didn't know we were all bloodline witches at the time.

But Isobel did.

"Why didn't you reach out to the other families?" I respond between sobs, attempting to pull myself back together.

They could have figured it out. Isobel had the answers.

Barrett's motions are controlled as he bends down to

assist me upright. I jerk away from him, stepping backward until I reach my friends, reclaiming my space between Jessa and Riley.

Tahlia leans across the group and hands me a tissue she pulled from her back pocket. I blot my eyes, awaiting Barrett's excuse.

"It's complicated," he begins. "After my dad told us the story, we attempted to reach out to Margo's mom, Mia. At that time, Mia was the only surviving ancestor of Lydia Bishop. Mia's dad died when she was a toddler—it was the curse. Her mother—a drug addict who overdosed when Mia was sixteen—left her bouncing through the foster care system. I couldn't in good conscience tell her and add to her stress. Then years later, she married Mark Hawley and—"

"My dad," Margo cuts him off.

I glance to Margo on the far end of our group. The pieces are falling together for her too.

"He died when I was little, leaving my mom in shambles," Margo says sullenly.

"Margo, we always kept an eye on you and your family; we made sure you were safe," Bree adds. "Your mom has never shown signs of magic, so it's safer if we keep it that way. Plus, I don't think she could emotionally handle it."

A disappointed expression settles on Margo's face. Margo knows that's true. Her alcoholic mother can't handle any of this.

"What about my family?" I demand. "Isobel wanted the curse broken. Why didn't you go to her?"

"How do I say this?" Barrett begins. "Isobel had a

reputation, and we didn't trust her. Associating with Isobel would have fueled the rumor mill, and we couldn't have that kind of attention on us. Why do you think you guys only told tales of Isobel when they could have just as easily been about you?"

"What about Anna or my dad?"

"We tracked down Anna, and to say she wasn't kind is an understatement. She threatened to curse us herself if we ever contacted her or her family again."

"Sounds like Anna," I respond.

"But soon, the curse was the least of our worries," Bree responds.

Tim lets out a maniacal laugh that rattles my nerves.

"Careful, or I will use those restraints." Bree pounces toward the cell, shaking her fist at him.

"I had a job to do. I had just turned eighteen, and I was ready to fulfill my duty. My parents trained me, then I found my first targets—a new witch and a traitor," Tim says. His words are a sick reminder that Riley's nearly eighteen.

"Clearly, you didn't succeed," I taunt.

"Not for lack of trying," Bree responds. "We were at war for many years, always on guard, never feeling safe. It was a stressful time. Then we had Callen, and we knew we couldn't live like this. We asked for a truce, even directing him to focus all his energy on the Beswicks, but he had a one-track mind. Thankfully, Tim found someone to occupy his time, shifting his focus for a while."

"Mom? Was she a hunter too?" Riley questions, throwing his hands in the air.

"Yes. Us hunters like to keep the bloodline strong—especially the originals." Tim tosses a shameful glare at Bree.

"What happened to your mom?" I ask, realizing I've never asked about her—ever. She's never been a part of his life as long as I've known him.

"She left. I don't know where she is." Riley's words are full of aching.

"Great, another hunter out in the world," I snap.

Oh crap. That's not the response a person should have when their assumed boyfriend tells them they've been abandoned by their mother.

Pain settles in Riley's eyes.

"I'm sorry," I mouth to him.

His expression doesn't change. I feel awful. I'm on guard, and every hunter poses a threat to me and my dad—the only Beswicks left. Will I ever be safe?

"Tim's wife Lauren was pregnant with Riley at the same time I was with Tahlia. Shortly after, Mia was pregnant with Margo. I knew this rivalry couldn't continue for the sake of our children. They didn't deserve this, plus it's a small town. So, we drew up a treaty. I made sure Mia and Margo were included—just in case. We all lived fine, going undetected, minding our own business, until you arrived." Bree glares at me.

I sense an unease in the air. Bree's making me uncomfortable. I need to get out of here.

"Well, I appreciate what you did today, but I think it's time I get home. My dad will be worried." I pull out my phone to check the time and notice I don't have a signal down here.

"OK. I'm sure your dad is looking for you. Remember, when Anna's body is found, you had no idea she was here. None of you ever saw Anna," Bree says. "Riley, you'll stay with us tonight. We need to work through the logistics of this situation. People will notice your dad's missing soon, so we need to get our stories straight. Callen, you'll drive the girls home."

"I want them to stay here with me tonight," Tahlia begs.

Bree nods. "Fine."

"I can't stay. I have to go home. My dad—Anna. I need to be there."

"I'll take you." Callen steps out of our lineup and leads me toward the stairs.

"And kids, none of this information can leave this room. Jessa, you're only included because of your earlier involvement. So, if you want to keep your friends alive, you won't say anything. Not even to your parents. You got it? Trust me; it won't be pleasant if Barrett has to force your mouth shut by magic," Bree says.

Jessa's eyes widen.

"So, what? Callen takes my place now in our circle?" Jessa whispers to Tahlia, but everyone hears her.

"No one is taking anyone's place. None of you are allowed to practice magic," Bree huffs.

"When four bloodline witches get together, no good can come from it. Look at your ancestors. Jealousy, greed, and death can fester among covens," Barrett adds.

I take a few long strides alongside Callen, ready to get the heck out of this place.

"Also, I'm going to need the spellbook. I saw it when we arrived." Barrett holds his palm out.

"It's mine." My hand involuntarily grips the strap of the bag across my chest.

"Izzy, you shouldn't have it. It needs to be kept safe."

"It will be safe. With me." I nod for Callen to keep walking.

I'm worried as we rush through the house. I carefully check over my shoulder, but no one is behind us. We make it to the SUV, and I still have my book.

A sense of relief rushes over me as I hop into the car. I place my bag next to me and yank on the seatbelt.

I'm almost fastened when there's a loud knock at my window.

I freeze, afraid to see who's come for my book. A surge of fear ripples through my body as fire courses through my limbs.

CHAPTER 06
LOVER BOY

Panic builds in my stomach as I twist my head. My eyes flutter rapidly, trying to gain traction to the silhouette outside my window. The angled sun constricting my view, mixed with a heavy dose of fear, has my mind firing off worst-case scenarios left and right.

Did Tim escape?

Did they send Sid?

Is Barrett here to pry my book away from me?

"Izzy," a familiar muffled voice calls out from the other side of the glass.

My nerves calm. It's only Riley.

I squint through the rays of blinding sunshine inconveniently descending toward the horizon. He motions for me to roll my window down. "You didn't say goodbye." His words are sweet with a hint of woe, making my nerve endings tingle.

Callen tenses in his seat. I'm not sure why, but my eyes jolt to him for approval.

He gently nudges my elbow. "Go ahead. Say goodbye to lover boy. But be quick."

I quickly glance toward Callen and flash him a giddy, closed-mouth smile before turning to roll up my window. With a gracious gesture, Riley opens the door for me.

"Such a gentleman." I blush as I feel the gentle pressure of his hand on mine, and he helps me down from the SUV.

He leads me to the side of the house, near the garden. The delicate scent of the fragrant flowers creates a much-needed moment of euphoria.

"It's a little more private over here. No prying eyes or ears."

A wave of heat rushes to my cheeks, and my lips curl up into an affectionate smile. I shyly glance down, fearing this moment could be our last before his hate turns his heart icy cold with disdain for me.

Riley pulls my chin upward, letting his baby blue eyes meet mine. "Hey, I know we're on borrowed time right now. But I can't—I won't end up like my dad. You have to believe me that I'm going to do everything in my power—"

"You only have a few more days," I cry out. "We don't have the first clue how to stop you from turning." I run my hand up his arm, stopping just below his jersey sleeve. My grip lingers on his masculine biceps before slowly pushing the fabric up. His tattoo has grown. It's darker, thicker, and more intricate than before. I gasp. "Riley . . ."

But Riley doesn't break his gaze. He doesn't need me to point out his fate; he already knows.

"For what it's worth, I'd really like it if you'd be my girlfriend. If things change in a few days, I'd understand if you change your mind, but right now, I—"

"Yes, of course, I'll be your girlfriend." I twist the fabric of his shirt and yank him close. Pressing my lips into his, I kiss him sweetly at first, then more zealously.

He pulls away, leaving his face just inches from mine. My lips quiver in his absence.

"Izzy, we'll find a way. I promise. We're supposed to be together."

"Riley, I hope you're right."

He places one hand on the small of my back and presses his body tightly against mine. He traces his finger along my face with his free hand before slowly twisting my head. His lips greedily move down my neck, his breath hot on my skin, adding to the fire that's already flaming hot inside me.

I relish the moment, letting Riley's lips cover my exposed skin. But that little voice in the back of my head is telling me he could snap at any second. I should pull away, as I'm being too vulnerable with my life. Yet, I don't move. For some reason, I trust Riley, even if I shouldn't.

His heart beats rapidly against my chest, nearly in sync with mine. For a second, it feels like time has stopped. I don't want this moment to end.

His lips slowly find their way back to my mouth. My body is now raging with fire, making me dizzy, but instead of pulling away, I playfully bite his bottom lip. A smile forms between our parted mouths.

"You better get going," he says, pulling away for air.

"I wish I could stay here with you."

"Me too."

The sound of Callen clearing his throat faintly makes its way to us.

"I think we have an audience," Riley whispers.

"Izzy, we really should get going," Callen calls from around the corner.

"I'm coming. Give me a second," I shout. "I'll meet you in the car."

"Everything is going to work out," Riley says, tucking my hair behind my ear. He kisses me on the forehead, then lovingly shoos me away.

I dizzily walk back to the driveway with a beaming smile.

"About time," Callen says as I slide into the passenger seat.

"Sorry, I should have said goodbye before leaving. I need to soak up as much time with him as I can before, you know . . ."

"I get it," Callen responds, keeping his eyes pinned forward.

"Hey, thanks for giving me a ride home."

"It's nothing."

"And I suppose I owe you a huge thank you for coming to our rescue today in the forest. If you hadn't come, we wouldn't have broken the curse. And things could have ended differently for everyone."

"I knew you needed me, so I came." Callen shifts the car into reverse and backs down the driveway.

For a brief moment, our gaze meets, and he offers a charming smile as he pulls onto the street.

"Was it hard finding out what you were—a half-breed?" I ask.

"Not really. It wasn't as hard for me as it was for Tahlia today. I also didn't have an audience or a dramatic scene leading up to it. I think I always knew there was something different about me. Then once I found out, I couldn't help myself. I dabbled—a lot. My dad doesn't even know what I'm capable of. So, that's our little secret."

"The glamour?"

He nods. "My parents don't know I can do that."

"What are you going to do about Jessa's Jeep?"

"I'll take care of it. You have enough to worry about."

I can't help but think of Jessa's Jeep parked in front of my house. I hope it's still glamoured, or we're all in big trouble.

"Don't worry, it will be fine for a few more hours," Callen says, interrupting my thoughts.

He always seems to know what I'm thinking, and I find that a little disturbing, but also comforting. It's like, for once in my life, I don't have to hide who I truly am because he just knows. He feels it.

Callen takes the last turn up the hill toward my house. "Hey, I know you think you're in love with Riley, but I don't think it's a good idea to get involved with him. I mean, further than the situation at hand. It's OK to be friends and want to help him, but hunters are good liars. He might not care for you like you think he does. Hunters can be manipulative to get what they want."

Anger slithers under my skin, and I get restless in my seat. "I don't think this is any of your business. I've known Riley since I was a kid. We have a history. You don't know what's best for me."

"He's a hunter, Izzy. If you think it will be like my parent's relationship, you're wrong. I hate to break it to you, but he's going to try to kill you every chance he gets."

"And what about your sister? Are we going to abandon her too, if she becomes a hunter?"

"That's different."

"How?"

"It just is. Trust me. Have I steered you wrong yet?"

"No, but we just met. You have plenty of time to disappoint me."

Callen shifts the vehicle into park, and I glance up toward my house. Every light is on. That's strange.

"Give me your phone," he says, passing me his. "We need to exchange numbers. You may not agree with me on certain things, but call me if you need anything—anytime."

I press my information into his phone.

"Izzy, your phone is blowing up with messages from your dad."

A rapid wave of guilt rushes through me. We didn't have service in the basement, and I was too preoccupied to even think about checking my phone once I was outside.

I anxiously wait as Callen finishes inputting his number. We exchange phones, and I click on the message icon. A slew of texts invades my screen.

Dad: Izzy where are you?

Dad: I'm getting worried about you.

Dad: I think we have a visitor. I think my mom's here!

Dad: Izzy, are you with my mom? Please text me.

Dad: I think something has happened. Please call me or come home now.

Dad: IZZY! Text me back.

"My dad knows Anna is here. I have to go. Thanks for the ride."

"Call me if you need anything. I'm serious."

I grab Tahlia's messenger bag and sling it over my shoulder. I glance down, noticing a few tiny drops of blood—Anna's blood—glistening against the car's harsh lighting. Once again, visions of Tim hovering over me with a knife flash through my mind.

"Hey, can I borrow your hoodie?" I ask Callen, leaning back into the car, pointing at the stains on my tank.

Callen has blood on his shirt too, but it's less visible in the thickness of the tightly woven fibers of his assumingly expensive hoodie.

"Of course."

He gives me a playful smirk as he releases his seatbelt. Callen wiggles out of his black hooded sweatshirt only to reveal he's not wearing an undershirt. He twists his torso toward me, handing over his sweatshirt. I can't look away; his six-pack of abs keeps drawing me back.

"Oh, I'm sorry, I thought you had on another layer."

"It's a little hot out for that, don't cha think?" He winks.

Our hands meet during the pass-off, and sparks flicker through my fingertips. Callen grins, and my face flushes hot. I must be blushing. How embarrassing.

"Are you sure it's OK that I take your only shirt?"

"Yes, Izzy. Quit worrying."

I slink out of the car and let Tahlia's bag slide down my body, then I tug Callen's hoodie over my head. It hangs long and awkward on me, but it will do. It smells like him, not that I've ever smelled him before, but now I know his scent.

I shimmy the bag back into position and pivot toward the stairs.

"Goodbye, Callen." I wave in his direction, avoiding eye contact in fear of my gaze wandering down to his shirtless stomach.

"Be safe, Beswick," he calls out as I lunge up the steps to my house.

The motion of twisting my key in the lock makes the pit in my stomach twist.

Can I face Dad knowing Anna is dead?

CHAPTER 07
AM I DEAD?

"Dad, I'm home," I shout, taking a hesitant step into the foyer.

Normally, the sight of unknown luggage in my home would be cause for concern, but I'm not shocked by the small, floral print suitcase standing upright beside the door. It's Anna's, and it's just where Bree said it would be—staring at me, taunting me.

It's another ugly reminder that I know what happened to Anna, and my dad doesn't. It's going to kill him when her body's found. He won't understand, but it's better that way. I must keep him safe.

"Dad!" I call out again.

When he doesn't answer, I pause to face the Victorian hall tree mirror, sickly hoping for something magical to happen. Something or someone to direct me through this mess. I haven't heard from Isobel or Anna since we broke the curse. Are they still with me? I close my eyes and listen—waiting for them, but nothing happens.

When I open my eyes, the gangly girl in the mirror wearing a sweatshirt two sizes too big stares back. Nothing strange here—a normal reflection. Except I'm a hot mess. I attempt to weave my fingers through my hair, but it's useless.

I bet I can make it to my room and change before I meet up with Dad. I honestly thought he'd be waiting by the door, cross with me for going hours without checking in or responding, ready to ground me. I guess all that can wait a few more minutes.

I'm about to leap up the staircase when a ravenous fire blazes through my entire body, paralyzing me in my tracks. I wrap my arms around my midsection and lurch forward in agony. I want to scream, but only tortured moans come out.

What's wrong with me? Am I dying?

My body drops to the floor as the fire inside me rages on.

I pull my knees tightly into my chest, willing the pain to stop.

Why is this happening? I haven't felt anything this intense before. It feels wrong. I try to fight back, but my body stiffens.

I'm a witch. I should be able to do something to help myself. I close my eyes, summoning images of a perfect body, one that isn't on fire, but my thoughts are unbearably clouded—getting murkier by the intense pain.

The fire swarms fiercer through my stomach.

My eyes darken as I get sucked into blackness.

***

Am I dead?

It seems like a valid thing to ask myself.

The tide of fire inside me has retreated, leaving me with a wave of nausea and light-headedness. My limbs twitch as I regain my movement. I pull myself to my feet, but I'm unsteady. I lean against the banister for support.

What just happened to me?

I'm about to warp into total freak-out mode when a flash of warm air stirs around me. I shift my head to see Dad walking through the front door. The invasion of humid air makes my stomach curl, and I want to vomit. I pull in a deep breath, pushing down the panic crawling through my organs.

Whatever *this* was, it has to wait.

It's game time.

I can't worry Dad more than I already have. I have to compose myself.

"Izzy, you've had me worried sick. I thought you might have gotten lost out back. It's not like you to ignore me."

"I'm sorry, Dad. I went out for ice cream with the girls after school. Then we got to talking, and I lost track of time." The lies slip off my lips easier than I thought they would.

"Plus, I think your grandma is here." He nods to the luggage.

I scrunch my nose. Dad knows I've never called Anna grandma.

He frowns at my expression. "Anna," he says, fixing his mistake.

My heart yanks because I would love to call her grandma now. She protected me, loved me, and saved me. My emotions are wavering, but I can't let them show.

"So, where's Anna?" Tingles of guilt pulsate through my body.

"I was hoping the two of you were together. I've been searching this entire house inside and out for both of you."

"And you left every light on. Dad, we're not made of money."

I'm doing a good job pretending, mocking my dad for things he gets on me about. Father-daughter banter is geared up for a full swing, but Dad doesn't play along.

"I keep trying her phone, but it goes straight to voicemail." He waves his cell phone toward me.

It's going to voicemail because she's been held hostage since Saturday, and now her body's lying lifeless in a creek waiting for hikers to stumble upon it.

"Maybe she went out for a walk," I suggest, thinking of her shoes by the back door—the ones Bree planted there.

"Maybe, but it's dusk. She should be back by now. I'm going to call Tim."

"Dad, she's a grown woman who we hardly see. I'm sure she's fine. Don't you think you're overreacting?"

The palms of my hands are sweating. I wait for Dad to look away before rubbing them on Callen's hoodie.

"I have a sick feeling something is wrong. Tim will know what to do."

I watch as Dad's fingers search for Tim's number. My stomach is growing queasier by the second. It will probably go to voicemail or just keep ringing, but I can't have him catching on to Tim's absence just yet.

"Oh, thank heavens. There you are," Dad says, tucking his phone into his pocket as he crosses the room.

"There who is?" I nervously question.

"Did you miss me?" a voice mutters.

CHAPTER 08
COMPLICATIONS

My chest constricts, and I'm having a hard time breathing. This must be a panic attack. The ground feels like it's going to open up below me and swallow me whole. I vigorously rub my eyes, but the image in front of me goes unchanged.

There's no way—it's impossible.

"Of course, I missed you. It's been years since we've been in the same room together," Dad responds.

Confusion ripples through me.

"Anna? How are you here?" My words scrape up my throat, coming out muddled and hoarse.

"I think what Izzy means to say is, what are you doing here?"

"I just wanted to see my family. That's all."

The tall, thin woman with long, gray wiry hair standing in my foyer is supposed to be dead. Her eyes are nearly translucent as she peers through me.

"Steven, this house looks awful," the woman says. Her movement is slow as she glides through the foyer, letting her gaze rest in every corner.

I saw her die.

She's dead.

We were together in the in-between world. But now she's walking through my house, fully alive—not dead.

My eyes narrow suspiciously on her, not letting her out of my sight.

"Isobel, you look terrible. Why don't you change your clothes and meet us for tea in the dining room? We have a lot to catch up on."

"It's Izzy." My ingrained response slips off my lips. But my unintentional blunder is perfect for going along with this ruse, for Dad's sake.

"I'll get the kettle going," Dad says, leaving the room, frowning at my rudeness.

The air in the foyer suddenly feels thinner as the gray-haired woman stares at me. I glower back, unsure how to proceed. This doesn't seem like the same woman who showed me images of her love for me earlier today. Her jaw tightens, making me tense and defensive.

"You should be dead." The words involuntarily fly out of my mouth.

Her thin eyebrows rise slightly. "Isobel, that's no way to talk to your grandmother. I'm sixty-three years young. I'm not going anywhere anytime soon." A bitter smile draws across her chapped lips.

"But—"

"Now go on, child. Go fix yourself up."

There's no mention of our afternoon in the forest—her death—nothing.

It's like today didn't happen.

I open my mouth to refute her, but she turns and strolls away without offering another word. I want to call after her, but my words don't come. Instead, fear has me rooted, and my jaw hangs agape in disbelief.

The weight of indecision is crushing me as I struggle to pick my next move.

Is it safe to leave Dad alone with that thing?

I can't tell my dad that his best friend killed his mother—the woman standing very much alive in my house right now. That sounds insane. Who would believe that?

Dad, this woman you call mom died just a few hours ago. I watched Tim stab her, then my friend's parents tossed her off a cliff. So, there isn't a chance in hell this woman could be here uninjured standing in our kitchen. But ta-da! Here she is.

Nope, it doesn't fare well when stated out loud or in my head. I can hear the doubt in my own words, as if I don't believe them myself.

What I *do* know is that I need to call for reinforcements.

I have no idea what I'm up against.

A sudden burst of energy inspires my feet to move, and my decision is made.

Inside my bedroom, my hand trembles as I attempt to create a new group message, one to include Riley and Callen too. I slink to the floor as my fingers linger over the keypad, trying to compose my thoughts to the group, but for some reason, I can't type out the words. Instead, I compose a different text.

Izzy: I need you. Can you please come?

Three little green dots immediately flash on my screen.

Callen: Of course. What's going on?
Izzy: Not over text.
Callen: Very cryptic!
Izzy: You said if I needed anything.
Callen: I'm already on my way ;)
Izzy: Don't make me regret this.
Izzy: Text me when you're here.

A wave of confusion washes over me as my phone slides from my hand, dropping to the floor.

I chose Callen over Riley.

Why?

Should I recant my text to Callen and message my boyfriend instead?

Yes, I should do that. Riley should be the one I call when I'm in trouble.

I reach for my phone, letting it rest in my hand as I stare at the blank screen.

No, it's too late. What's done is done.

I toss my hands up in frustration, overwhelmed by the sheer complexity of my life.

Things have gotten way too complicated.

Who am I kidding? I moved past complicated the day I arrived in East Gate. I slide the bag of complications off my shoulder: a spell book, a diary, and a knife that killed the woman downstairs. Yup—way past complicated. And now I'm texting a boy that isn't my boyfriend for help. When will I stop tossing myself into the fire?

With a deep breath, I haul myself to my feet, knowing my items need a new home—and soon—because of that thing downstairs. The real Anna knew about the hide-a-hole upstairs, so that's no longer an option—just to be safe.

I scan my bedroom, searching for a good hiding place. Maybe Barrett was right. Perhaps he could keep the book safer. The thought irritates me.

Of course, I don't have any ideal hiding spots. Ugh. I wish I had a large walk-in closet full of shelves and drawers right now. Since I don't, I stuff the bag under my pillow and fluff the other side to match the height. I guess this will do for the time being.

Now, what should I do? Do I change my clothes as requested, and exchange pleasantries with a dead woman over tea, while I wait to sneak Callen into my house?

My thoughts sound insane, but I suppose that's my next step. What other choice do I have?

I swing the door of the wardrobe open. My fingers glide through my hangers before pulling out a purple T-shirt and a pair of linen shorts. Callen's hoodie easily slips over my head. I toss it and my bloodstained tank in the hamper.

My fresh clothes feel nice against my skin. I wish I had time to shower, but this is better than nothing. I run a brush through my hair, focusing on the tangles as a distraction from what's waiting downstairs for me.

A text from Callen comes through as I'm finishing up.

Callen: Here.

Izzy: Wait five minutes. Front door's unlocked, let yourself in. Sneak in. Steps to the left. Second floor— last room. BE QUIET.

Callen: OK

Izzy: I'll meet you when I can.

In the dining room, Gran-gran's tea kettle is on a trivet in the center of the table with three white teacups neatly placed in front of each chair. I take a seat at the far end and reach for the kettle.

"Set that back down. It's still steeping," Anna scolds me as she comes in from the kitchen with a box of crackers in her hand.

Dad follows behind with three small plates that match the cups. I've never seen them before. We don't use fancy dishes—ever.

"Don't worry. It's decaf." Anna checks her watch. "One more minute."

And two more minutes until Callen sneaks in.

"Mom was just telling me about her drive here. She stopped at a museum yesterday and stayed in a bed-and-breakfast in Philly before finishing her drive."

Lies. All lies.

"That sounds nice. What museum did you visit?" I play along.

"Oh dear, you don't want me to bore you with that," Anna responds.

That's because you didn't go to a museum yesterday. You were here.

The creak of the hinges on the front door causes me to tense in my seat. I loudly clear my throat several times, drawing the attention toward me, not the boy sneaking into our home.

"Are you OK?" Dad asks.

I cough a few times before responding, "Just a frog in my throat."

"Good thing it's time to pour the tea." Anna reaches for the teakettle and pours a small amount into each cup. She opens the box of crackers and tilts the box toward me.

"No, thanks. I'm fine with just the tea."

She frowns and passes the box to Dad. He eagerly takes a handful and sets the pile on his plate.

"So, how long are you staying with us?" I ask, glaring at her.

"I haven't decided."

I want to call Anna out on her lies, but I shouldn't until I talk to Callen. He saw her body in the forest. He knows she's dead. Maybe he can explain this to me. He seems to know a lot.

I wish I could tell my dad the truth. I'm not sure withholding this massive secret from him keeps him safe. But the consequences of him knowing could be worse. I'm walking a fine line here.

Parents are the ones who are supposed to keep their children safe, not the other way around.

I guess that means Anna won't harm her child. But what if this isn't Anna?

I know Anna doesn't want my dad to know about the magic for his safety, but she's acting as if that conversation never happened. She's treating me like before she found us in the forest.

How is this my life now? Second guessing who occupies the body of my dead grandma is my new hobby.

I take a small sip of my tea, then discreetly spit it back into my cup. I forgot I hate tea. This stuff is nasty. I'd rather have coffee.

I stretch my arms above my head, letting out a fake yawn.

"It's been a long day. I think I'm going to head to bed and let you two catch up. I'm sure you have a lot to talk about."

"Izzy, are you sure you can't stay up a little longer?" Dad questions.

"I'm beat."

Dad's head tilts toward the table, letting a frown hang long on his face.

"It's all right, Steven. Izzy needs her sleep." Anna reaches out and rubs her son's hand. The sight of her tenderness makes my stomach coil. The real Anna wouldn't do that.

Who or what are you, Anna?

I push myself away from the table, ready to excuse myself, when Anna grabs my wrist.

"It's OK. We can catch up tomorrow."

My arm goes cold from her wrinkly touch. The icy chill travels up my arm, freezing me to my core.

Anna and I burned hot when we touched in our in-between world.

This isn't Anna.

CHAPTER 09
FREAKSHOW TEATIME

Callen's sitting on the edge of my bed, facing the doorway, when I barge into the room. My breath is labored and panicky. The sight of him isn't helping either. I chose him over everyone else. Why did I do that? Was it the right choice? My world is already so messed up, why not layer on the fact I summoned a boy to my room that's not my boyfriend?

Intuition—a gut feeling. That's what told me to do it.

"What's going on? Why am I in your bedroom? Not that I'm complaining." A sly smirk tugs at the corners of his mouth.

Ugh, and he's so darn hot. Which is so *not* helping the matter at hand and the guilt that's swirling through my stomach, making me nauseous. Is it wrong that I'm disappointed he's wearing a T-shirt, covering up his handsome muscles?

Izzy, stop it. You're taken now.

The impostor in my home is my number one priority, not this.

Get a hold of yourself, girlie.

My eyes slowly gaze over every inch of him before letting my words slowly release, since they sound insane inside my head.

"Anna . . . She's here."

He doesn't react right away, but gradually, his velvety eyes melt with confusion as his brain spins to put my response into something comprehensible.

"Wait. What?"

"Anna showed up." The words sputter out of my mouth.

"Like someone found her body?"

"No, Callen, like something awful happened to me when you dropped me off. I felt like I was dying, then moments later, Anna was standing in my home—very much alive." Saying the words out loud makes me wonder if the two incidents are connected.

"I felt something earlier, but I couldn't pinpoint the distress. I'm so sorry. I thought it could have been you, but the feeling was clouded, and you've been so clear to me. But Izzy, that's impossible. She was dead. I saw it with my own eyes. Plus, don't you think my parents would have noticed if she were alive when they tossed her body off a cliff?"

"If you don't believe me, sneak downstairs and see for yourself. She's having tea with my dad right now. Fucking tea!" I shout. "And she hasn't mentioned anything from today—like it never even happened."

"I'm sorry. I want to believe you, but I must see this myself."

"Be my guest." I wave him toward the door. "But don't get caught. I need you to stay in this house with me tonight. I can't be alone with that thing in my home." My voice is sharp and assertive.

"You're coming with me." He yanks me out of the room and gently tugs me through the hallway.

We tiptoe down the staircase, with every other step creaking on the way down. Each noise jolts me into a panic, and I freeze in place like it's going to stop the sound from carrying into the dining room. Thankfully, Dad is too preoccupied with his mother, whom he hasn't seen in years, and we make it to the foyer without commotion.

We post up on opposite sides of the doorway that enters the dining room, where the freakshow teatime is occurring.

I serve as lookout and gesture with an awkward hand motion when the coast is clear. Callen sneaks a glance, and as he pulls his head back around the wall, his mouth falls open, and his eyes widen.

I shoot Callen an *I told you* so expression as I sneakily cross the threshold. I yank him away from the unfathomable spectacle in my dining room. He doesn't close his mouth the entire walk back to my bedroom.

"Now, do you believe me?" I ask, locking the door behind us.

"Izzy, what the hell was that?" He pulls in a few shaky breaths.

"I don't know. I hoped you'd be able to tell me."

He rubs his temples. "I have no clue. But Anna was dead." Confusion settles heavily across his forehead as he paces the room. "Let's say hypothetically that Anna didn't actually die in the forest. Well, then, why hasn't she brought any of it up to you? It seems like something she'd want to discuss at great lengths. She'd want to make sure you were safe—from Tim and Riley. Right? I mean, she's not that heartless, is she?"

"Great question. We were alone for a moment, and she had her chance. It's like it never happened. I had a tender moment with her right after she died."

Callen stares quizzically at me, making me feel insane. Did I dream the whole thing? No—I didn't. I was there with Anna after she died.

"Remember when you told me about the limbo world where witches live in the in-between?" I pause to suck in a dose of courage to continue. "I was there with Anna right after Tim stabbed her with the knife. She showed up, and we touched. Anna showed me things—things that only she would know. She was kind to me there, nicer than she'd ever been. She told me she kept me at bay to protect me, and that she loved me, and she'd always be with me. But now I don't hear her. I feel like she's lost."

"She's not lost. She's downstairs having a casual tea with your father. But Izzy, I've never heard or read anything about any other witch crossing into the limbo world—really, it's another realm. You'd have to be mighty special for that to happen. Are you sure you were there with her?"

"Yes, and I've been there before. But by myself. On my first day here, I fainted and was transported to a linear timeline, just like with Anna. I could move around freely, and no one could hear or see me."

"Seriously?" he questions.

I can't tell if he believes me.

"Yes," I sternly respond, trying to direct the conversation back to the matter at hand. "But the Anna in the other realm was nothing like the Anna that's downstairs."

"Maybe she doesn't remember," he offers. "What if she only died momentarily? Like you could only speak to her because she was in a death-like state. Then my parents tossed her body, which banged her up a bit in the head, but she woke up. Maybe we all thought she was dead, when she wasn't."

"Are you saying it could be like amnesia from the fall? That seems far-fetched," I respond.

Callen strokes his chin. "Farther fetched than a witch dying then coming back to life?"

"Good point. None of this makes logical sense."

"Nope. It sure doesn't. We're pulling at strings here to make sense of something that's impossible." Callen spans his arms out, letting his body flop backward onto my bed as if he's admitting defeat already. "I should call my parents."

"No, you can't. What are they going to do at this hour? It's getting late, and they can't show up now. My dad will question things. We can't have him find out about any of this. He can never know what he truly is—a bloodline witch. It's the only way to keep him safe."

Callen sucks in a deep breath, holding it in for a few moments before loudly letting his inflated breath escape. "I suppose it can wait until morning."

A wave of relief rushes over me. "OK, good. So, now that we've established that you're spending the night, and we're waiting until morning to tell everyone, we should probably get to work. In addition to the newly added stress of the Anna situation, we still have a curse to break, remember?"

"You never stop, do you?"

"We can rest when this nightmare is over."

"Can I ask why you didn't call lover boy to help with Anna?" He repositions himself on the bed, now sitting upright.

His question intensifies my guilt, making me regret my decision. Everyone will soon be aware of my slip in loyalty.

"He has a lot to deal with right now. I can't add to his stress."

"What about the girls?"

Also, another good point. My friends have been through this whole mess with me. My girls are my girls.

"I think I've put them through enough today." My response is generic because I don't know the reason. I messed up, but there isn't anything I can do about it now. What's done is done.

"So, you don't care that I've also been through a lot today? Remember, I've been running around all over town, covering up and fixing your messes all day."

An involuntary giggle slips, and I playfully respond, "Nope, you seem pretty durable. I thought you could handle it."

"I suppose you're lucky we crossed paths when we did then."

I offer him a kind smile. "In all seriousness—I am."

"Good. I'm glad we met too. Even if you're a pain in my ass, Beswick." He grins.

"So, what do you propose we do tonight?"

He wrinkles his nose. "Magic, of course."

CHAPTER 10
ELEMENTAL MAGIC

I study Callen's face from across the room. Is he serious? Does he want to do magic with me? Is that really a good idea, given everything that's happened in the past few days? My heart races from the excitement and fear that's battling inside me.

"I want to teach you some useful tricks. You need to learn responsible magic. The basics. Things that can help you when you're in a bind."

"Like the glamour?" I excitedly question.

"Sure, we'll work toward that. Come sit." Callen pats the space next to him.

I crawl onto my bed, then cross my legs. Callen pivots his torso to face me, while resting one knee on the comforter and letting his other leg dangle off the bed's side.

He places his hands out, palms upward, gesturing for my hands, and I set them inside his. My body roars with a fiery shock, but a good fire—the one I'm used to.

I wiggle from the interaction but leave my hands in place. "Can I ask how you know so much? Did your dad teach you?"

"No, I'm self-taught. My dad never wanted me to practice unless necessary, in fear of being found by other hunters. We had the treaty with Tim, but others are out there just waiting for us witches to make a mistake. Plus, he told me I'm useless without a coven. But I could feel the tide of magic swirling around inside me. I knew he was wrong."

"Oh, wow. And you didn't have a spellbook? How did you know what to do? Like with Sam Hornsby and the toxicology report?" I ask excitedly.

"No spellbook. Just instinctual magic. I thought our ancestor's book was long gone. But apparently, Isobel had the original this whole time. Which you now have. I thought the book was just a myth. So, without any guidance, I had to get creative, learning on my own through lots of research, and I began creating my own book of shadows."

"Book of shadows?" I question, wondering why it sounds familiar.

"It's a place where witches record their spells and rituals. Mine is like Isobel's but much smaller."

Ah, the spellbook. It was written on the first page.

Thy Book of Shadows belongs to High Priestess Isobel Beswick.

"When something works, I write it down. But most of my spells are so intuitional that I don't need them in words. I simply remember because of the feelings they stir inside me."

"Wow, that's really interesting. Do you need candles and other items?"

"It helps, but it's not necessary. Remember the story my dad told us about our ancestors escaping? They pulled from the earth's gifts. Since your bloodline is purer than mine, you should have no problems conjuring the powers needed, even when they're not close."

"See, I'm glad I called you. You know stuff." I grin.

A genuine smile falls across his flawless brown skin.

"Can I tell you a secret? Something I haven't told the girls," I giddily ask.

"Of course."

"I unlocked a door and lit candles with my thoughts." I bite on my bottom lip to hide the prideful gleam that's trying to sneak across my face.

"So, you're not as novice as I thought." He winks.

"I imagined what I wanted to happen, and it did."

"A true witch."

"I suppose so." I beam with excitement. "So, what's the plan here?" I wiggle my fingers in his hands.

"Concentrate," he responds.

I quiet my thoughts and focus solely on Callen and our shared space. Just like in the car this morning, my hand vibrates in his. Energy circulates between our palms. It's intense. It's weird. It's emotional. My lips quiver. A single tear plummets from my eye, but I don't move to wipe it away.

"Izzy, we have something special between us. Before meeting you, I'd never connected with anyone else like this. Not even my dad. Nothing this intense has ever happened to me before."

I bashfully glance down at the bedding, sensing my cheeks reddening. "I feel special."

"You should." His voice is soft.

I allow my eyes to meet his piercing, dark gaze.

"You have such a unique eye color."

"I've been told that." He chuckles, pulling his hands away, freeing me from his vibrations. "Hey, can I ask how you knew where to position everyone in the circle? I'm assuming you were the one who assigned everyone." His brow rises slightly.

"It was a gut feeling."

"What do you know about elemental magic?"

"Nothing, but I have a feeling you're going to tell me."

"Yup. Time for your first lesson." Callen pulls his leg up to join me in sitting cross-legged on the bed. He doesn't look very comfortable, but I let him continue maneuvering until he finds the right spot. "Each of the four elements has a guardian or watcher. Every witch connects with one of the elements: earth, air, fire, and water. When you invite these guardians into your circle, they become your protector. I've always identified with water, and that's what was left for me today."

"That's where I had Jessa, and you filled her place."

"Interesting. I think something was intervening long before we even knew. The water guardian is my protector and has been since I began practicing. Water is the gut reaction, the emotional response, and the wave of energy that tides through me."

"That just gave me goosebumps," I admit.

"There's always something bigger than us at play. You're fire, right? I could feel the momentum of the flames rushing through you before you even called on your guardian today."

I shake my hands out at my sides like he touched a nerve. That's eerily accurate.

"Since the moment I stepped foot in this house, it's been a part of me—the fire. I couldn't tell if it was good or bad."

"Izzy, it's your radar—your meter. It's everything all at once. Fire is the most volatile element. It moves with the energy inside of you, guiding you. Fire is said to have birthed the other elements, giving them life. It makes sense that you've been gifted fire, since you're the purest bloodline. You're our high priestess. It's what makes the most sense."

"What do you think about Tahlia and Margo's stationing? Did I get them right?"

"I think you hit the nail on the head. Tahlia is the most level-headed of the group. She's grounded and resilient. She's tough and strong. She's earth—at least for now."

"I don't want to imagine her changing into a hunter. Your mom seems to carry herself with grace, but then I look at Tim, and he's a monster who can't control himself. I'm surprised he went all summer without attacking. I can't think of Tahlia being like that. But I think she's going to be a witch. I feel it. I can't let any other outcome happen. We need to make sure of it. We need her. She's one of us."

I think back to Anna whispering into her ear, keeping me safe—the good Anna, not the imposter Anna downstairs. Tahlia was open to her messages, which gives me hope.

"We have some time to figure it out," Callen says.

"But Riley—"

"Hey, not now. Let's not go there."

I nod, knowing he's right. It's useless to keep getting worked up over the same thing. "So, Margo—air."

"Air is special. Air is everywhere, making it a powerful

element. Some say it's the predictor of the future. Air sees things coming because it's all around."

"Wow, that's Margo. She knew we were all going to be friends. She said it out loud. The book called to her, showing itself to her first. She led us into the forest and directed us during our first spell."

"Dang, girl. Big things are at play here. Magic is all around. Maybe it wasn't just your ghost witch granny leading you to your calling."

"Maybe. It's so crazy—all of this," I respond. "So, does that make Margo psychic?"

"I don't think you could call it that. From what I've read, it's an intuition thing, but how Margo decides to process her information is up to her."

"That could be useful. Can I tell you something else?"

Callen nods.

"You're not anything like I thought you'd be when we first met."

"A whole twelve hours ago." He laughs.

"Hey, don't forget the coffee shop, Mr. Barista." I giggle.

"You're right. How could I forget that moment with extra everything?"

"And the moment we connected for the first time." I grin at the thought. "We've been through a lot together in our short friendship. But I have to say, I think we're kindred spirits, you and me."

"Agreed." He smiles.

"So, are we going to do some more magic or what?" I ask.

"First things first. We must keep your dad safe while

dealing with the hunter's curse. We need to perform a protection spell. We don't know what we're dealing with when it comes to Anna coming back from the dead or whatever happened to her. Better to be safe than sorry."

"Without Tahlia and Margo?"

"It's an emergency. They will understand."

"I mean, are you sure we can do something of that capacity without them?"

"Absolutely."

"Do you know a spell, or should we use Isobel's book?"

"Let's see what the old book has to say about protection spells, shall we?" Callen suggests.

I tug the comforter down and toss the pillow on the floor.

"Great hiding place, Beswick," he jeers.

"I work with what I have."

I pull the heavy book from the bag, and Callen's eyes widen like a kid running free in a candy store. I lay the book in the space between us.

"Wow, so this is it? The Wives of Salem Coven's Book of Shadows." He flips it open. "It has an energy around it."

"You know the book zapped Jessa when she touched it. It should have been our first sign that she wasn't like us."

"Izzy, that's another lesson. If something like that happens, you have to follow it. You could have avoided the whole ordeal with Jessa by not including her in the first place."

"Try telling that to Jessa. She's a pushy one."

"That she is."

Callen's eyes fall back to the book. His eyes gleam as he flips each page. "Do you realize these spells are ones that

Isobel, Elizabeth, Dinah, and Lydia personally tested and committed to ink? This is so cool."

I let Callen continue turning pages until he lands on the final passage. "Undoing The Witches Bloodline Curse," he says, reading the top of the page. "Did you notice this spell was added much later than the rest? Isobel must have been working on perfecting this spell for years before committing to writing it down. She didn't have all the necessary things required to break it, but you did. And it worked. She knew you would figure it out, Izzy."

"And I did. We did."

I give Callen a few more moments to ogle over the book. It's a lot to take in, and he has a different appreciation for it than we did at first glance.

"It's pretty impressive, isn't it?" I ask.

"It's amazing, Izzy. The high priestess usually guards the book for the coven. Isobel was the keeper of this book, and now it's you, because you're her kin. Don't let my dad get a hold of this sacred item. I can't help but feel he would destroy it. Not out of hate, but out of his willingness to protect us. You need a much better hiding spot."

"I know. I'll figure it out, so until then, I'll keep it with me."

Callen points to an open page in the book. "Ah, here it is." He runs his hands over the entry. The ink darkens as it did for me, but this trick doesn't faze him. He's used to his magic working when needed.

I glance down at the open book resting on my bed, sitting between two bloodline witches. My body tingles with excitement.

A Spell for Protection
We call upon our guardians to protect (name)
We ask that you bind and shelter (name) from harm.
Keep a watchful eye and avoid alarm.
We call upon thee to protect (name) with love.
May your protection wrap (name) like a glove.
Guardians, be blessed, and be with us through our grace and greed.

So shall it be.

"This is it." He grins. "Now, we need to create a circle for our protection."

I frown. "All of my supplies were out in the forest, and we can't sneak upstairs to Isobel's circle and chance getting caught."

"Anything will work. Get creative."

I leap off the bed and rummage through my room, searching for something useful. I pull open the top drawer of my vanity, and a white spool of thread stares up at me.

"Does this work?" I flash him the spool.

"That will do. Toss it." He holds his hand out.

I awkwardly fling the item in his direction, but he craftily maneuvers to catch it.

"Since we don't have any elements near us and are down two witches, I need you to focus all your energy on each element. Visualize them as we call upon them together. It also helps to imagine a white light. White is the color of protection. Don't ever forget that one. It may come in handy when you're alone," Callen says, using the thread to create our circle on the slippery hardwood floor. Then we'll chant the spell three times."

"OK. I got it."

"What's your dad's name again?"

"Steven."

Callen and I step inside our homemade circle, careful not to ruin the loosely made protection Callen created with a simple piece of thread. We drop to our knees. He gently sets the spellbook in the middle, where we can both read from it. He takes my hands, and the vibrations strum fiercely through our encompassment.

Instinctively, we both draw a deep breath and begin on the exhale. I imagine a glowing white light of protection surrounding my father. The rapid movement of the water behind our house flows across the imagery flashing through my mind. I embody and give thanks to the air I'm breathing and the fire that runs hot through my veins. I envision the earth, where I gathered strength from earlier today.

"Earth. Air. Fire. Water," we chant three times.

The vibrations from his energy ripple through my hands and into my body. It's the most beautiful sensation I've ever experienced. My heart races, and my pulse quickens. My dad's safety is riding on this spell working. I imagine him fully embraced by the security this spell offers. The fire inside me roars and rapidly whips through us in a wild, repeated circle. Callen flashes me an amused grin that warms me more than the heat racing through my insides.

Callen nods to the page, indicating it's time to begin. We recite the words in unison.

We call upon our guardians to protect Steven Beswick.
We ask that you bind and shelter Steven from harm.
Keep a watchful eye and avoid alarm.
We call upon thee to protect Steven with love.
May your protection wrap Steven like a glove.
Guardians, be blessed, and be with us through our grace and greed.

We repeat the spell twice as the air grows purer around us. Nothing crazy happens this time. There's no random wind or things stirring around us, but it feels right.

Our lips press out the final words, "So shall it be," closing out the spell. Our hands stay locked around one another as we stare intensely into each other's eyes. My stomach flutters. I know this can't continue. This isn't the magic; it's us. I let my hands drop, and Callen's expression falls flat.

"Do you think it worked?" I ask.

"Does it feel right inside?"

"Yes," I respond.

"Good, me too."

Callen stands, stepping outside our ring. "I'm getting sleepy. Do you care if we call it a night?"

"Wait. You're leaving me?"

"Oh, no. I just think it's been a long day, and we'll do much better tomorrow if we have a good night's sleep. Magic can be exhausting; you need your rest too."

"Sure," I respond, knowing darn well I won't stop searching tonight for a way to break the hunter's curse. "But you said you were going to teach me some basic tricks. I feel a little cheated."

"Tomorrow. I promise." His eyes scan the room. "Do you have some extra blankets? I can sleep on the floor."

"On the hardwood?"

I didn't think about where he would sleep when I asked him over.

"Callen, you can't sleep on the hard floor. I can share my bed. It's huge. I fit all the girls on here with me, if you can believe it."

"I don't think your boyfriend would like that too much."

"It's OK. We're just friends, right?"

He rubs the back of his neck. "Of course, just friends."

The gleam in his eyes dims like a light slowly going out.

Does Callen want more from me? Sure, we have an undeniable connection, but that's because of the magic—kindred spirits.

He sulks to the other side of the bed, where he flops himself on top of the blankets. I yank the book up and place it on my pillow. I lay on my tummy so I can read comfortably.

"Is the light going to bother you?" I question.

"I'll manage. Night, Beswick."

"Good night, Callen," I whisper.

CHAPTER 11
COLD SHOWERS

The sunlight rudely invades my room, warming me more than I'd like. I can't bear to open my eyes, not yet, at least. I need a few more minutes to pull myself together before facing the day and the boy in my bed.

A chaotic mixture of last night's events mingles through my mind. Each memory tugs for my attention, tormenting my brain as it fights for its place in my recap.

The protection spell—did it work?

Anna—is she really here?

Callen—did I disappoint him last night? The magic between us is undeniable. But that's it, right?

Riley—Tahlia—the curse. Can it be broken?

Why did I choose Callen over Riley and the girls last night?

Each thought circles through my brain like a high-speed carousel, nearly making me dizzy. I have only four days until Riley's eighteenth birthday. The curse should be my only concern, but now it's not. I'm in a web so twisted I wonder if I'll ever find my way through it.

In another reality, one where hunters and witches don't

exist, I would be doing normal new girlfriend things like obsessing over whether to buy my boyfriend a gift, since we just started dating, or deciding about whether to throw him a party.

But that's not my world.

In my world, hunters and witches are real and so are the burden of the curses they carry. My world involves people coming back from the dead and hot boy warlocks who aren't my boyfriend sleeping in my bed. My world involves magic spells of all kinds—dark—light—and even gray.

I squeeze my eyes tightly, wishing my complications would fade away, but I know it's useless, just like Isobel's book of spells. I was silly to think I would find something to undo the hunter's curse. That curse wasn't placed until Elizabeth banished the witches, and the only addition to the book since 1692 was the undoing of the bloodline curse. It was also the only page to mention the hunters—Isobel's entry, where she warned and instructed me to kill all the hunters.

Maybe that's why Isobel's not talking to me. I failed her. But what does she expect? I can't kill them all. There are too many out there. I'd rather focus on breaking the curse, instead of being a murderer. I'm seventeen, ready for college, not a life in jail.

So, why did I think I could find something lingering between the pages? A spell doesn't exist, and Elizabeth Crowley succeeded. Isobel knew the only way to rid the world of hunters is by death.

I can't accept that, though.

There must be a way.

There's always a way—I hope.

A thought creeps into the forefront of my brain, nagging me. If The Wives of Salem Coven could create their own spells, maybe we can too. I'm a bloodline witch with a coven, so why can't I do the same? We need our own Book of Shadows and maybe even a catchy name like The Witches of East Gate Coven—I like the sound of that. Well, that's as long as Tahlia doesn't turn into a hunter; otherwise, I might need to recruit Barrett as our fourth, and I'm not excited about that one bit. He doesn't jive with us and he's old. So, another reason to break this curse. We need Tahlia.

I stretch my arms above my head, wishing I could lie in bed all day and tuck this nightmare that's my reality away, but the brightness trying to break through wins the battle, forcing me to confront the fears whipping savagely around my mind.

My eyes flutter open against my will and immediately scan for Callen, searching the bed up and down.

He's gone.

Callen left me.

Abandonment stirs inside me, making me confused and angry.

He said he'd stay.

He lied.

My body jolts upright with terror invading every cell inside me.

"Where's the book?" I ask out loud, expecting a response from someone or something, but no one answers—not Isobel—not Anna, and not Callen—silence.

It's unnerving feeling so alone. I haven't felt this alone in months. I suppose I took comfort in knowing something was always with me, even if I couldn't explain it. Now, being alone feels like a limb is missing. A piece of me is gone. Where did Isobel go? Where did her guidance go?

The book—I must have fallen asleep reading it last night. It was here next to me on my pillow. I know that for sure. I toss the pillows off the bed and hastily explore the sheets, but it's gone.

Did Callen take it?

Did Anna sneak in last night?

This can't be happening.

I leap out of my oversized bed and cross the room, frantically skimming every surface. Relief settles over me as I spy the spellbook sitting neatly on my vanity table, along with a piece of paper on top.

My book is safe.

I grab the note. It's from Callen. He didn't abandon me.

Izzy,

Good morning. Sorry I had to leave. Don't be mad. I had to take care of something important. I don't think your friends can give you a ride today. Stop by The Perk on your walk to school, and I'll make you an iced mocha with extra everything ;)

Callen

Be safe.

Well, now I can't be mad at him—extra everything. That

was sweet of him to leave a note, but what did he mean by—

The gears churn in my head, slowly clicking into place as I rush to my windows. Gaping down at the street below, I notice something is missing—Jessa's Jeep. Callen must have snuck out last night to deal with it. I can't imagine what he did to make it disappear. Magic or something lawbreaking?

I reach for my phone to text him when a message from Jessa comes through.

Jessa: Swinging by to get my jeep in a little while. See you soonish.

I let my finger hover over the screen but decide not to message back. It's best Jessa discovers this on her own. I abandon the idea of texting Callen too. I'll see him soon. Plus, I need to hurry and get ready, or I'll be late for school again. If I'm tardy a second day in a row, the school will question why. I wasn't close to Megan, so I can't keep using her as an excuse.

Just as I'm about to set my phone on the table, Riley's name illuminates my screen, and my heart thumps with anxiety from last night's decision.

"Hello," I hesitantly answer, my mouth suddenly dry.

"Izzy, I just wanted to hear your voice."

When I hear Riley's voice on the other end of the line, my body aches at his melancholic and fragile tone.

"How was last night?" I ask.

There's a long pause. "Hey, I got to go. There's a lot going on around here this morning. I just wanted to say good morning." The line goes dead, and I'm left with a hollow unease that I don't know what to do with.

***

As I shower, letting the hot water stream down my face, I try to wash away my nagging thoughts surrounding Callen and Riley. I have more pressing matters to deal with, like keeping my dad safe from Anna. I hope and pray that our protection spell works. I'm putting blind trust into a spell I can't test without putting my dad in harm's way. I can't fathom something happening to my dad. The magic has to work. It must keep him safe from Anna—whatever she is. People don't just come back from the dead.

If this spell doesn't work, am I really as powerful as everyone says I am? Callen can do some intense solo magic, so I should be able to do it too. That whole fourth-generation witch thing should work to my benefit, right? I shouldn't need Callen or my coven. Standing in my old claw-foot tub turned modernish shower, I let that thought overcome me.

Solo magic—I need to try again—I need to know what I'm capable of on my own if it comes down to it. I must know if I can protect myself and my dad.

Time to test the waters, so to speak. I close my eyes, imagining the dual crystal-looking knobs; one labeled H and the other C, twisting as far right as they can go. The water that slinks down my skin gives me a jolt, not like an electrical shock jolt, but more like a euphoric sensation that penetrates my cells, vibrating under the skin.

Water isn't my element, but it seems to work with me, playing off my intentions. There's a charge surrounding me, swirling with the stream. I press my eyes tighter, imagining the shower head slowly drawing all the water molecules back inside.

It's working.

The water pressure is pulling back.

Oh, crap!

"Brr!" I shiver.

A burst of icy cold water flashes my skin, sending a chill to my bones. I flip my eyes open, disappointed to find only the hot water knob twisted as directed. I quickly yank the cold-water handle to the off position, ending my little experiment. My trust in my abilities is wavering.

The fluffiness of the blue towel I'm wrapping around my body is the only comfort I find in this moment. Let's hope my magic is more potent with Callen, and we can keep my dad safe. I lock my badgering thoughts of failure securely away in the back of my mind. I need confidence to move forward.

"I'm Izzy fucking Beswick."

"I'm a fourth-generation bloodline witch."

"I'll keep everyone I love safe."

"I can do this."

"I am magic. I am fire. I am me."

Feeling pretty good after my self-induced pep talk, but now pressed for time, I blow-dry my hair on high heat. I add some loose curls and dab on a little extra makeup, focusing on my eyes to hide the puffiness from my lack of sleep. I slip into a pair of frayed jean shorts and a loose T-shirt that hangs off my right shoulder, exposing my lacey bralette strap. Shoving my feet into some basic black flip-flops, I call it good.

If Jessa's not outside already, she should be arriving soon. With that thought, my phone rattles next to me. I don't have to look; I know it's her. I strut over to my window. She's already frantically pacing the empty parking spot where her car should be, having the exact reaction I predicted.

I hate keeping secrets from my friends, but Jessa *did* hit Megan. I can't ignore that fact. Megan is dead, and the murder weapon—the Jeep—must be destroyed to keep us safe. As Callen said, it's not just about me now. It's about all the bloodline witches and even the hunters, at this point. People can't find out about us. East Gate wouldn't know what to do with us, and I'd hate to see what they'd come up with as punishment. History tends to repeat itself.

I shudder at the thought.

Jessa's flashing her phone and shouting at someone. I crick my neck to catch a glimpse of who she's lashing out at. Riley, Margo, Tahlia, and Barrett are also here. I thought this would be a single-person event or a Jessa and maybe one of Tahlia's parent's kind of event. I didn't expect to see the whole crew this early in the morning. I also thought I'd have more time this morning to prepare myself for Riley.

All right. It's game time. I got this.

I grab my backpack, tossing the diary and spellbook inside, leaving the knife in Tahlia's bag. I can't take a weapon to school, so I tuck the bag between my box spring and the mattress for safekeeping until I get home.

Outside, I'm greeted by a panicked Jessa, along with the rest of my friends. Jessa's wearing a black strappy tank, clearly one from Tahlia's closet. It's the first time I'm seeing her wear a dark color. It doesn't fit her style, but Jessa's outfit faux pas is the least of our problems.

"Izzy, you better not be messing with me." Panic ripples through Jessa's voice as she crosses in front of the group, flailing her hands in the air at me.

"Why would I mess with you, Jessa? Your Jeep was here when I came home last night. I don't know what happened to it. Honest."

Half-truth.

"I'm calling the cops!" Jessa shouts. "Someone stole my fucking Jeep."

Barrett calmly pulls Jessa's phone from her shaking hand. "That's not a good idea. We need to get Tim's truck out of here first. Then you may call the cops." Barrett slips her phone into his back pocket.

Jessa huffs out a forceful breath. "Fine."

I frantically scan the area, searching for the familiar sight of Tim's cherry-red truck, but I don't see it. I step off the curb, the pavement rough and rocky beneath my thin flip-flops as I gaze down the block.

"It's parked down the side street," Riley says, startling me.

I turn and crumble at the sight of my boyfriend. His disheveled state is much worse than I imagined, from his red-rimmed eyes to yesterday's dirty clothing hanging wrinkled off his body. I want to swallow him in my embrace and tell him everything is going to be OK, but I don't know that it will be. Plus, guilt claws at my heart, keeping me from wholly being there for him. I'm off to a great start at this whole girlfriend thing.

Riley rocks on his feet, balancing over the curb. He rubs his hand anxiously over the back of his neck. "I rode here with him yesterday. My car's at school. He parked down the side street, so you wouldn't notice when you came home. I'm sorry, Izzy. I don't think I can apologize enough for yesterday."

"I'm sure being here stirs up emotions, but you don't have to worry about me. You were just doing what your dad directed you to do. He's the monster, not you."

"Not yet."

"Not ever. We'll figure this out."

"So, are you going to school like that?" I question, but my words come out wrong.

"No, I'm not going. Bree had my dad call the school and tell them I'm sick, then she made him call the station and tell them he's come down with a bug. So, I need to take his truck home before anyone sees it and questions our story. Then I'm heading back to their house."

"Oh," is all I can say.

"I think they want to keep an eye on me," he whispers into my ear.

His words send a flicker of heat through my body.

"Hey, what's going on out here?" My dad's voice sneaks up from behind us.

"Dad!" I shout awkwardly.

"You must be Mr. Beswick," Barrett says, walking toward my dad, not offering his hand to shake.

Either Barrett is a germaphobe, or he's afraid to let his magic touch a Beswick's magic. He didn't shake my hand, either.

"Yes. That's me. Izzy's dad. You can call me Steven." My dad's enthusiasm comes off sweet, but it's a little much for this group right now.

"I'm Tahlia's dad, Barrett. Nice to meet you." He nods, staying in his controlled form like some kind of soldier, keeping his hands idly by his side.

"Great to meet you too. So, what's the commotion out here?"

"Steven, someone stole my Jeep. Have you seen it?" Jessa asks in a whiny voice, running up toward my dad.

Gag me.

"Sorry, Jessa, I haven't seen it. Riley, maybe you should call your dad. He'll know what to do."

Riley pinches the bridge of his nose and directs his gaze to the ground, clearly avoiding eye contact. "He's sick today. I shouldn't bother him," he says, refusing to look up.

Gosh, my boyfriend is a terrible liar. He's going to get us all caught.

"Oh, that's a bummer. I hope he gets better soon. Tell him if he's not feeling up to it on Sunday, not to worry about stopping by. I have a visitor, anyway."

"A visitor?" Barrett questions, his voice rising at the end.

Everyone else falls obediently silent by Dad's words,

stopping dead in their tracks, waiting for him to continue—to correct his statement—that he *thinks* he has a visitor.

"My mom is here." His statement is blunt and said with certainty.

"Oh, that sounds nice." Barrett's brows tighten with a sheen of sweat seeping into his creased forehead.

Dad turns and waves up at the house. "Mom, come down here and meet Izzy's friends."

My dad's gesture causes a ripple effect through everyone on the street. Jessa's keys fall from her grip, clanking as they hit the pavement. Barrett's mouth hangs wide open as Margo loops her arm through Tahlia's, tugging her close. Riley practically falls off the curb, taking long strides backward until he runs into me. He reaches his hand out for mine. I lace my fingers between his, and the chill from Anna's presence keeps the heat from working its way up my arm.

The gray-haired thing calling herself Anna glides down the cement steps, taking them leisurely, leaving everyone in suspense. Her thin lips press into a flat smile as her translucent gaze widens, taking in the sight of all the witches and hunters standing on the sidewalk. Most of whom she's already met—well, the real Anna met them.

This will be interesting.

My dad rushes over to meet Anna on the final step, taking her by the arm over to the group. The sight makes my stomach coil.

"Mom, meet everyone. This is Jessa, Tahlia, Margo, and—"

"Riley Hawkins," Anna says, cutting Dad off.

"Yes, Tim's son," Dad says.

"I remember, Steven. I couldn't forget a Hawkins." Her words are ice cold, causing Riley to tense up beside me.

"Izzy, I'm disappointed you rushed out of the house this morning. I thought we were going to catch up," her words sound hollow and unconvincing.

"Um," I begin to say, but she already has her eyes set on her next target.

She twists her body, almost instinctively. "And you, Barrett Hart, right? I don't think we've officially met. How's that wife of yours?" A wicked smile draws across her face as if she's taunting him.

Barrett's dark golden skin pales at her words. I can tell he's trying to keep his composure. If my dad wasn't standing here, I think things would be going differently right now. Barrett's glare sharpens. "Nice to finally meet you in person, Anna. My wife is good," he says with a clenched jaw.

"Well, Mom, we should let Izzy and her friends get to school. Jessa, do you need me to call the cops about your car? I can't believe someone stole it from outside of our house. I didn't think things like that happened in East Gate."

Jessa's face is frozen, but she manages to shake her head from side to side.

"I'm sure it's one of their friends messing with her," Barrett says. "I'll take care of it. It was nice to meet you both."

"It's very nice to meet all of Izzy's little friends," Anna says, pausing on her way back to the stairs. "Oh, and what is this?" She swipes her finger between Riley and me.

My dad shifts his gaze down to our interlocked hands.

"It's new," is all I can say.

Anna's face furrows with disappointment—not that I care what she thinks. My dad's face, on the other hand, is hard to read, but that's not something I can deal with right now. My face reddens in embarrassment, but the flash quickly passes as they finally maneuver toward the steps.

Barrett takes a couple of long, controlled strides until he's right in front of my face. He waits until Dad and Anna are behind the closed door before addressing me. "Izzy, you must tell me what's going on?"

"Anna showed up last night. She just waltzed into my house like nothing was wrong." I pull in a shallow breath. "I thought you said she was dead."

"She was dead. I'm positive. There's no mistaking that—I mean, I think. No, she was dead." Barrett rubs his temples vigorously as if he's searching for clarity in this situation.

"Well, clearly, she isn't dead," I respond.

"Dad, how is that possible?" Tahlia asks.

"It's not, sweetheart. It's not possible." Barrett puts his hand over his mouth and shakes his head in confusion. "I've never encountered anything like this before. It doesn't make sense."

"When are things going to go back to normal?" Jessa whines. "I'm over this whole witch thing."

"You're the one who started this whole witch thing," I respond under my breath.

"OK, here's the plan. Jessa, call your parents about your car. They can deal with this. Then you girls get to school. Riley, I'll follow you to your house. We'll drop the truck off; you can shower and pack a bag. Then we'll discreetly pick up your car at school after class begins. Riley, Bree, Sid, and I will work on things, including our new Anna problem. Everyone is invited for dinner at our home tonight, and not coming isn't an option."

"OK," we all agree in unison.

Jessa holds her hand out, waiting for Barrett to produce her phone, then walks away with it firmly pressed to her ear.

Riley gently kisses me on the forehead. "I wish you would have called me last night." He turns away, disappearing behind Barrett's Silver Lincoln Navigator, giving me no time to respond, and leaving me with a brick of guilt weighing me down like an anchor. He doesn't even know the half of it. I glance back to the street to see his messy hair bobbing up and down as he jogs around the corner to his dad's truck.

Sorry Riley.

"We should hurry, so we can get to school," Margo says, eyeing the clock on her phone. "Not that we don't have more important things going on in our lives right now."

"Right," Tahlia responds.

"I could go for some caffeine on our way. Can we stop by The Perk?" I'm taken aback by the words that come tumbling out of my mouth. My subconscious is one sneaky little bitch.

Even with my guilt anchor weighing me down, I still can't stop bobbing with the current that's already whipping me around.

But instead of waves, it's boys.

And it's not caffeine I need at The Perk—it's Callen.

CHAPTER 12
LIFE, DEATH, AND JEEPS

After Jessa's call with her parents, we walk to The Perk. For the briefest of moments, it feels normal—the four of us walking shoulder to shoulder down the middle of my street toward downtown. Just four friends grabbing a coffee before school. Nothing strange about that. Without any spoken words, we appear ordinary to the outside world. Well, maybe slightly above ordinary. I mean, look at my friends; they're gorgeous, intelligent, and popular. But ordinary humans at first glance.

Once our mouths open and our words are in the air, all that changes—our façade is shattered. We aren't four high school students walking to school. We're four unusual beings—witches, half-breeds, cursed, murderers, and witnesses to multiple crimes. It's good that we have each other, or we would have nothing.

"Why didn't you call us last night?" Tahlia asks. "When Anna first showed up?"

"I'm sorry. I didn't want to worry you."

"Are you insane? We would have worried, and we would

have been there in a heartbeat. Riley too," Margo says.

"I know, but I felt it was best to wait until morning. I didn't want to alarm my dad. I had things under control." I don't spill the beans about Callen. I wonder if they noticed he was gone last night.

"I get it. But next time, don't hesitate to reach out, at least. Even if we're going through our own shit, we'll be there for you," Margo responds, grabbing my hand.

I keep my blocker up to avoid her getting into my thoughts. Although I can feel hers—fear and sadness. She's worried about her mom, wondering if she has any clue that she's a witch.

"Right, girls?" Margo says, coaxing Jessa and Tahlia for a sympathetic response.

I squeeze Margo's hand tightly, but quickly let it drop, fearing she will accidentally sync up with my frequency.

"Yes, of course," Tahlia agrees, but she's distracted with her own problems, and I get that.

With Jessa's head buried in her phone, I wonder if she's heard any part of our conversation.

"Hey, what do you think of this color? Is it me?" Jessa asks, looking up from her phone, flashing us a picture of a brand-new black Jeep.

Well, that answers my question—self-absorbed much?

"My parents weren't mad. They said it was probably stolen, and they'll turn it in to our insurance or whatever they have to do. I bet I get a new car out of this whole situation."

"Really, Jessa. That's what you're worried about right now?" Tahlia shrieks. "What fucking color of Jeep you're getting next? You're a spoiled brat. Don't you care that I just discovered I'm a half-breed?" Tears flow over her high cheekbones, soaking her face and ruining her foundation.

"I thought we talked this through last night?" Jessa responds.

"Talked it through! Jessa, you've got to be kidding me. This isn't something I'll get over in one night. If I'm a witch, I might be OK with that, but how can I live with myself if I'm a hunter? I can't turn into a monster like Tim. What if I can't control myself and try to kill Margo or Izzy? Jessa, this is life-and-death we're talking about. This is our friendship at stake, and you're worried about a stupid Jeep."

"We all have our problems, T. I'm suddenly not in the mood for coffee. I'll meet you at school." Jessa flips her platinum blonde hair over her shoulder and struts away, abandoning us outside The Perk.

"Are you kidding me?" Tahlia tosses her hands in the air. "Did that really just happen?"

"She's just pissed that she's not special." Margo props the coffee shop door open for us, caressing Tahlia's back as she walks through.

"What I wouldn't give to not be special right now." Tahlia softly pats her face with the palms of her hands, trying to control the tear induced mess.

Thankfully, only a couple of people are in the coffee shop, and most appear to be leaving. Although, the people lingering stare at Tahlia with concern. I try to flash the onlookers a pleasant smile, but they shift their gaze to the floor, suddenly aware of their noticeable intrusiveness.

"I'm using the restroom. I'll be right back," Tahlia says.

Callen's enigmatic eyes radiate when they catch mine. Behind the counter, he's pouring a shot of espresso into a to-go cup. He holds a finger up and mouths, "Just one moment."

With intuitive behavior, Margo and I choose the same path and plop down on our chosen couch; a cozy green love seat in the middle of the café, just off the right side of the espresso bar with our backs to Callen.

Margo's eyes fill to the brim with guilt as her quivering lips open, ready to spill her feelings. "Izzy, I don't know where to begin, but I'm so sorry about everything."

Margo is the last person who should say sorry, but I know she's an empath, and she feels strongly when others have pain. I can sense that about her. "You have nothing to be sorry about, Margo. I should be the one apologizing to you."

Her eyes flutter with curiosity.

"Your life got flipped upside down the moment you became friends with me. The second you invited me to sit with you at lunch, your whole world changed. It's something I wish I could take back. If I had kept walking and chose another table . . ."

With her gaze shifting to a narrow slit, all her features pull together tightly in a serious expression—one I've never seen from her before. It's unnerving.

"Never ever apologize for that again. Do you hear me?" She rubs my shoulder.

I sullenly shake my head, letting my loose pieces of hair cover my face in shame.

"Izzy, I'm so glad you're here. I know the circumstances are strange, but me and you—we're like sisters—sister witches—or something like that. I can't imagine not having you in my life now that you're here. We've been destined to meet our whole lives. You complete us."

Guilt wraps around my organs, twisting them tightly until I can't breathe—*Megan.*

A burst of movement stirs around us as Callen glides my drink through the space between Margo and me, interrupting us, but catching my wandering thoughts, shifting them at the perfect time.

Callen, my hero.

"Did someone order a large iced mocha with extra whipped cream and extra chocolate sprinkles?"

"Aw, thank you, Callen." I twist on the sofa and offer him a grateful smile. Sparks flicker through my fingertips during the handoff, making me giddy inside.

Kindred spirits. That's all.

"No fair. Make me one of those," Margo pouts.

"Coming right up, but I only get one free coffee per shift, so I have to make you pay. Sorry. Plus, my boss is in the backroom; otherwise, I might not care as much. And I'm already on thin ice for being late yesterday."

"Oh, never mind," Margo says, hanging her head.

"It's OK. I got it." I hand Callen some cash I pull from my backpack, hoping it's enough to cover it.

"Be right back with your change and Margo's drink," Callen says.

"That's some excellent service," I joke.

"Wait, Callen." Margo tugs on his arm, yanking him downward, closer to us. "You missed a lot this morning. Anna's alive."

"She is?" he questions, but he doesn't sound shocked.

"You don't seem freaked." Her mouth twists. "You already knew, didn't you?"

"I'll let Izzy explain. I need to start your drink, or you'll be late for school."

Callen mouths to me as he backs away, "Psychic." He points at the back of Margo's head, then shrugs his shoulders, making me laugh inside.

"Izzy, tell me how Callen knew?"

I bury my chin in my neck. "I called him last night."

"You what?"

"Don't be mad."

"I'm not mad, but don't you think you should have called Riley, at least? He told us that you two made it official last night. Side note: I'll need the details on how that whole thing went down. But Riley's your boyfriend, not Callen."

"Once again, I didn't want to worry anyone. Especially Riley. His dad's in a cage, for goodness' sake."

"Izzy, you need to be careful. It's a small town, and people talk."

"I'm pretty sure I already knew that."

"Is there something going on between you two? You seem awfully close."

"No, just two friends who found out they're bloodline witches. Just like you and me. Just two friends—that's all."

"Hey, did you guys order me one of those?" Tahlia says, glancing at my cup as she approaches us with a fresh coat of makeup. "What are you two gossiping about? Riley?"

"Yup. Riley. He's my boyfriend now. Did you hear?"

I stand up from the couch. "Take my seat. I'll get you a drink too."

"Thanks," Tahlia responds. "Oh, but no whipped cream, no sprinkles, and maybe light on the mocha, and make it a small. Oh, and non-dairy too."

"So, no to everything good. Got it." I laugh, walking away.

Callen studies me as I approach the counter. "Your sister wants—"

"A boring, gross drink. Coming right up."

I wrinkle my nose.

"I know what she likes, or more, I know what she doesn't like, and that's anything with flavor," Callen explains.

I giggle at his joke, but I wince as I produce my last ten-dollar bill. But it's worth it as it buys me some much-needed alone time with Callen.

"Hey," I whisper, calling him back to the register. "Where did you go last night?"

"It's best you don't know."

"But the Jeep?"

"Nope. My lips are sealed. If you don't know what happened to the Jeep, it's one less thing for you to hide from them." He nods to the sofa.

"About that . . . I've been thinking. Could we find a spell to keep my thoughts and feelings to myself?"

"I don't like that idea, Izzy." Callen steps away, grabs a small cup, and pumps a single pump of mocha into the glass.

"Callen, why?" I move along the counter, trying to follow him.

He pours oat milk on top of the mocha, then he preps the espresso machine, ignoring me.

"Callen, please."

He nods for me to move back to the register.

"Here's your money back for Margo's drink. I got it, both of them." Callen hands me back my money and yanks out his wallet, tossing some cash into the register. "I know you don't have a lot of money right now."

I raise my brow, questioning his knowledge, but I know how he knows. Callen always knows.

"Izzy, that's why I don't want to do a spell. We're connected, and that's how I'm keeping you safe. If we do a spell, I could lose that power. Then what if Riley turns and tries to hurt you, and you need someone, and no one can hear you? That would kill me. So, no spell. Just be careful with your thoughts, OK?"

"Fine," I huff.

Callen walks away, pours espresso shots over the milk, lids it, then tries to hand me both drinks. I avoid his touch, making him leave the cups on the counter.

I wonder if he can hear my thoughts right now.

I have my blocker up; I have my blocker up.

You can't hear me; you can't hear me.

Nah-nah.

"What are you? Twelve? That's not nice, Izzy," Callen says, responding to my childish thoughts. "This isn't a joke." His forehead wrinkles with his lips producing a tormented frown.

"We should get going," Tahlia says, leaping up from the couch, reaching for her drink in my hand.

I pass Margo hers, along with a straw.

Callen leans across the counter. "Hey, girls, I get my car back from the shop this afternoon. I can pick you all up from school. I have a place I want to take you."

"Cool. Sounds good," Margo says, excitedly.

"Also, not sure if you heard, but Dad wants everyone at our house for dinner tonight. We have a lot of things to discuss," Tahlia says.

Callen nods. "Another interesting evening at the Latham-Hart house."

"Hey, where are you taking us later?" Margo asks.

"It's a surprise," Callen says with a playful wink.

CHAPTER 13
MRS. JAMISON

The school bell echoes loud and obnoxiously, warning us of our impending tardiness. Margo, Tahlia, and I flash through the open door where our teacher is stationed—waiting.

"Just by the skin of your teeth, girls," Mrs. Jamison lectures, narrowing her gaze on us. "Take your seat, so we can begin."

Tahlia rolls her eyes. "We're hardly late," she whispers under her breath as we cross by the front row of desks.

Mrs. Jamison clears her throat, pulling my attention back to her. "Actually, Miss Beswick, can I see you for a minute?" She gestures to the door. "Everyone, flip to page 242 in your textbook and begin reading. I'll be with you all in just a moment."

Fidgeting, I follow the thin-framed woman wearing a pencil skirt into the empty hallway.

Displeasure rests heavily on her face. "Izzy, I'm not sure you're adjusting well to your new surroundings, and I wanted to check in. Yesterday you missed class, and today you were tardy."

"It was like twenty seconds," I snap back.

"Tardy is tardy, Miss Beswick."

"What about Tahlia and Margo? Why am I the only one out here?"

"You're new. I don't want to see you slip through the cracks, especially during your senior year."

I bite my tongue, afraid I'll let a rude remark slip. How dare she? She doesn't even know me.

"I made a call to your old school in Seattle—"

"You what?" I interrupt.

"I was worried."

"I don't think that was necessary."

"Well, I wanted to make sure this wasn't a pattern."

"I can assure you it's not a pattern." I stare at her wide-eyed, waiting for a plausible response, one that makes sense. Because right now, none of this makes any sense. Who does this woman think she is?

"I know. After speaking with your former principal, who said you were a studious student, I can't help but wonder why you're acting out."

"Acting out? What are you talking about? I missed one class because my friends needed me. There isn't any reason for concern. And today, I was hardly late. I don't think I deserve this attention right now."

"I just want you to succeed, that's all. So, I expect you to be the model student you were in Seattle." She pauses, and her face flashes with an impish restlessness. "Terrible about that girl—your friend?"

"Who? Megan? We weren't friends—I mean, I didn't get a

chance to know her before she . . ." My words linger in the stagnant air between us. There's no need to finish that sentence.

"No, at your old school. The one who fell off a cliff. That's awful what happened to her. And well, I guess now that you mention it—Megan too. So much tragedy in such a short time," she says, slowly flipping her thick, bouncy chestnut-colored hair over her shoulder, stirring up a coconut scent that reminds me of Sondra's shampoo, making me nauseous.

Heat rolls under my skin, pulsating like tiny pinpricks.

"It's a lot for a young person to deal with." She purses her lips, studying me.

When I don't respond, she leans in. Her dark hair falls forward, wafting her coconut scent around us again, until I feel wholly overcome by it. I try not to breathe it in, but it's an impossible task.

"You know nothing like that ever happens in East Gate—well, that is until *you* arrived. Bad luck must follow you, Izzy. It seems you're cursed, my dear." Her words hiss off her red lips.

I jerk back, and my mouth drops in shock. Did she really just say that to me?

No, that's crazy. I must have imagined it, just like the skateboarder, Sam Hornsby, and Billy Drake. They never said the words I thought I heard. It was all in my head, or a witch in my ear, or whatever. It wasn't real, and neither is this.

I subtly shake my head, trying to dislodge the insanity once again. Staring straight-faced, I wait for her to repeat herself, but her brown eyes flicker with concern instead.

"Sometimes events can trigger other behaviors. It's best to nip them in the bud." Her voice is rigid with worry.

OK, maybe she didn't say it. My mind is playing tricks on me again.

Pull yourself together, Izzy.

"I'm fine. There's nothing to worry about," I respond with a controlled voice.

"OK, I'll trust that if there's anything bothering you, you'll reach out. And my door is always open. It doesn't have to be school related stuff, either."

"Thanks. Can I go back to class now?"

"Sure." She scrunches her narrow nose. "Oh, one more thing."

Her words catch me mid-stride.

"I could have sworn I saw your grandma recently. Is she visiting?"

I flip around, gazing at her with surprise. "Who? Anna?"

"Yes, I could have sworn I saw Anna Beswick in town."

Shit. Shit. And triple shit.

But wait. How does Mrs. Jamison know Anna? Anna hasn't lived here since my dad was born, and she hardly visits. Mrs. Jamison is younger, appearing to be in her early-thirties—maybe.

"I'm confused. How do you know Anna?"

"I told you I knew Isobel, so I knew *of* Anna."

"How?" I demand.

She blinks a few times, taken aback by my boldness. "We were friends."

"My Gran-gran didn't have many friends. Aren't you a little too young to be her gal pal?"

She fusses with the waist of her skirt and presses her

hand down the inseam, tensely flattening the fabric. "I was married." She pauses, drawing in a long breath. "My husband died six years ago. Isobel was kind to me and helped me through my grief."

Dead husbands and Isobel, that lines up.

"So, yes, Izzy. She was my friend."

"Oh." I'm not sure what else to say, so I plaster on a fake sympathetic grin and nod, hoping this is the end of our conversation.

"So, Anna? Is she in town?"

Dammit.

"I'm not sure. I haven't been home much," I respond.

So many lies.

I lie all the time now.

I guess it's my new thing.

Mrs. Jamison frowns, motioning for us to head back inside the classroom. I'm grateful this conversation is over, but now I'm left with a heavy dose of paranoia.

Could Isobel have shared her most guarded secrets with her? Everyone assumed, and rightfully so, that she was a witch. But when it came down to it, they were just rumors and stories as far as anyone could confirm. Did Mrs. Jamison ever question Isobel? Was Isobel weakened by her loneliness only to slip and let Mrs. Jamison in on her secrets?

No, that's ridiculous.

I shake away the thought. Isobel wouldn't have been that careless. She knew what was at stake if people found out about her—the real her.

Margo and Tahlia eye me carefully, searching for signs of

distress. I shrug my shoulders. Now isn't the time. I can fill them in later.

"Sorry for the delay, class. Today we're going to discuss the Salem witch trials."

You have got to be kidding me. Can't a girl get a little escapism, even at school?

***

My stomach lurches as I enter the cafeteria. Students are still gossiping about Sam Hornsby and commiserating over Megan. The incident is so fresh you can feel the wound breaking open and bleeding out over and over again. It's bad enough Megan died, but Sam's involvement makes it much worse.

But it could have been us on the chopping block.

Callen did what he had to do to keep us safe. To keep our kind hidden. But still, I wish there was something I could do for Sam. He had his demons, but he's going to pay for so much more. The school has turned him into a monster—a creature of nightmares. He's the boy you never should have trusted. He's the kid who hung out with football players but couldn't get the girl on his own, so he resorted to drugging them. He's the boy who overdosed his friend and let her wander away to die—cold and alone. He's the scum of the school, the town, and the state.

But did he ever really drug a girl, or was he just a dealer?

How much did Riley know of Sam's bad habits? Either way, Sam's little part-time hobby was wrong. The outcome produced a scapegoat, and Sam unknowingly took the fall for us. He was sacrificed for the greater good of our coven, and I must make peace with that.

What's done is done.

As I walk by Megan's friends, I overhear the details of her funeral. Wednesday—Catholic church—three in the afternoon.

Has Margo heard yet? Will she go? Are we expected to go with her? I don't think I can bear another funeral—my mom's was hard enough. I missed Sondra's—I wasn't wanted there, obviously.

Margo's alone, waiting bright-eyed at our table. She's so resilient. I admire her.

I take the seat next to her empty-handed.

"Aren't you going to eat?" she asks with concern.

"The food here is terrible, plus I don't have much of an appetite."

She slides her plate of french fries between us. "Here, you need to eat something. It's going to be a long day if you don't."

I smile at Margo's thoughtfulness. She's one of the most selfless people I've ever met. She'd give me the shirt off her back if I needed it. Even though the fries look soggy, I take one and dip it into the off-brand ketchup and shove it into my mouth.

"Have you talked to Jessa since this morning?" she asks.

I shake my head. "No, you?"

"No. She won't respond to my texts, either."

"Hey, Margo, I wanted to ask if you've heard about Megan's funeral arrangements?" I reach over and touch her arm, but quickly pull back so she doesn't feel my emotions.

"Yes, I'm going with Tahlia after school tomorrow. I'm sure Jessa will come, but I don't know yet. I know you want to be there for me, but you don't have to come. I'm sure funerals are hard for you since your mother . . ." Her words drop off.

Is she generalizing, or can she hear my thoughts?

No, I've been careful, keeping everything guarded, like Callen said.

I flash her sympathetic eyes. "I do want to be there for you, but I—I just can't. At least you'll have Tahlia by your side. She's a good friend and I know she'll be there holding your hand through it all."

"Izzy, don't worry. I totally understand. And yes, I'm lucky to have Tahlia." Margo's gaze is trained straight ahead, her expression distant, seemingly lost in thought.

"Are you worried about Tahlia turning into a hunter?" I softly ask.

She lets out a deep sigh, her eyes heavy with sadness. "I'm terrified. I can't imagine a world where a witch and a hunter can be besties, if you know what I'm saying?"

My head drops as I stare at the limp french fry in my hand, not sure what to do with her words.

"Oh, shit. I'm so sorry. I didn't realize what I was saying," Margo says, covering her mouth. "You and Riley can make it work. Look at Bree and Barrett. Tahlia will find a way to be our friend, and hell, she has a fifty percent chance of not being a hunter. But we won't have to worry about Tahlia or Riley turning because we'll figure it out as a group. I know we will. We beat the bloodline curse with pure dumb luck, so just think about what we're capable of now."

"I hope you're right."

"Shhh. Incoming." Margo nods to Jessa and Tahlia, who are heading our way.

The girls place their trays down and silently drop into their respective spots. You can tell neither one of them has opted to apologize first.

"So, what was up with Mrs. Jamison this morning, pulling you out of class like that in front of everyone?" Tahlia asks.

I roll my eyes. "She's a piece of work, that one. Would you believe that she had the audacity to call my old school? She was worried about me missing class yesterday."

"Are you serious?" Tahlia bursts in with a defensive tone. "That bitch needs to mind her own business."

"Agreed. And there's more." I pause to shove another fry into my mouth. "She was friends with Isobel. Apparently, six years ago, Isobel helped her get over her dead husband."

"Do you think we need to worry about Mrs. Jamison?" Margo asks.

"I really don't know. I used to think she was a harmless teacher, but now who the hell knows?" I toss my hands in the air.

"Do you think Isobel told her things?" Tahlia presses.

"For all our sakes, let's hope not," I respond.

Jessa moves a few things around on her plate but refuses to look at us. "Hey, my parents need me after school. I'll meet you at your house later," she says softly, then gets up and walks away.

"Tahlia, you need to fix things with her," Margo pleads.

"I'm not apologizing, if that's what you mean. She isn't being a good friend right now. The three of us have so much shit going on. We've lost loved ones, seen people die, and found out things that are beyond this world. She's just lost her car—that's it. She needs to apologize to us for being so snotty and aloof to our issues."

"I get that, but don't you think she might be going through more than just losing her car? She almost died yesterday too. She found out every single person close to her is something special, and she's probably afraid of losing her friends. Even if she has a funny way of showing it," I respond.

"You might be on to something, Izzy," Margo says.

"Tonight, before dinner, we need to make it right. We need to show her we care about her too and that she's still one of us," I add.

"Fine," Tahlia responds.

I stand up, slinging my bag over my shoulder. "I better get a head start to class. I can't have a second teacher breathing down my neck."

CHAPTER 14
INVOKE AWAKENINGS

I nervously await Callen's arrival as I sit on the cool cement steps in front of East Gate High. Tahlia and Margo join me, taking a seat near the bottom of the staircase. Jessa continues past us without so much as a single word, just like my last two classes with her, but I know we'll see her later. She won't abandon us. We're all in this together, even if she's not a witch or hunter.

None of us talk about our impending evening, or Callen's surprise excursion, because there are too many classmates lingering around. Everything we need to talk about these days is for our ears only. So, instead, I tensely eye the clock on my phone, wondering if I should stop home to check on Anna. My dad must have left her alone when he went to work. He wouldn't have thought anything of it. And why should he? Everything is normal as far as he's concerned. But leaving her unattended means she could be snooping. The thought makes my skin crawl. But now, after a little distance from the situation, part of me wonders if we all thought we saw something we didn't. Maybe Anna's simply suffering from amnesia, and she didn't really die. If that's the case, I'm being one rude relative. I told her she should be dead. Who says those things?

"Callen's here," Tahlia hollers toward me, knocking me from my thoughts.

I'm not shocked when he rolls up in a shiny black Cadillac SUV that's just as nice as both his parent's vehicles. Maybe Tahlia should have agreed to that part-time job if these are the kinds of cars her parents are handing out.

Geez. If I had that option, I would jump on that in a heartbeat. She'd have a nicer car than Jessa. I wonder if she's thought of that. Some kids don't understand how good they have it until it's gone—like me. I never knew what it could be like with less until it happened.

I toss my bag onto the black leather seat and hoist myself into the car, choosing the seat behind Callen. His velvety eyes glimmer, catching on mine through his rearview mirror.

I let out a long pent-up breath as I slam my door shut. "It's been a day!" My words fly out of my mouth as if they've been trapped there all day, waiting to escape.

"You're telling me," Tahlia agrees. "How can we focus on school when we have real-life problems we're dealing with?"

"Right," I respond, agreeing with Tahlia. "I can't stop thinking about Anna being all alone in my house and what she might be doing. Callen, do you think we can swing by and check on things?"

"That's not something you should worry about right now. My parents are on it. Trust me, they're keeping an eye on the situation."

"Are you sure?" I question.

"Have I steered you wrong yet?"

"Well, no."

"You did give my mom permission to enter your home, correct?"

"Yes."

"Then you have nothing to worry about."

"Eh, what does that have to do with anything? I'd expect her to break in if necessary."

"Well, that would be a little impossible if she didn't have permission."

"What?" Margo and I simultaneously question, stirring in our seats.

Callen chuckles as the three of us stare quizzically in his direction, waiting for a response.

"Hunters need to be invited in."

I giggle in amusement, assuming he's messing with us. "I think that's a vampire thing. You might be a little confused, Callen."

In the mirror, I see Callen cock his head to the side, and his features shrink into a serious expression. "Vampires aren't real, Izzy. But where do you think the myth came from? All myths start from somewhere—from a story passed down and changed to fit the fears of the people hearing the tale. Over time, the hunter became the vampire because vampires are scarier to the masses. Hunters are only frightening to witches. But this particular myth is true in some form. A hunter must be invited into a witch's home."

I rock restlessly in my seat, letting his words linger for a moment, thinking back to the first time Tim entered our house. My dad tossed him his keys and gave him free rein of our home. Bree directly asked for my keys and permission to enter my house, and my sweet Riley, he asked me if I was going to invite him inside.

Holy cow, it is a real thing.

I poke Tahlia in the arm with my pointer finger. "Hey, remember the first time you were at my house, and you didn't come in right away? I thought you were scared, but do you think you weren't allowed—because of the hunter's blood inside of you, keeping you from entering?"

She twists in her seat to face me and rolls her eyes upward like she's recalling the moment. She pauses for a few seconds. "Oh my gosh, you're right. I can't explain the feeling, but it was like I couldn't continue through the entryway. Like there was a barrier keeping me from entering. Then once you invited me in, it was as if I was nudged to keep going. I didn't put any thought into it until now."

"Even you, Callen. I texted you to come in. Not sure how much hunter blood you have in you, even so, your story checks out."

Margo slides into the middle and sticks her head over the center console. "OK, I have to ask, which one of our ancestors certified that spell?"

"Great question. I have no clue. It could have been any coven that's been hunted. But we should be thankful because it could save our lives one day," Callen says.

"That's a pretty big spell. If there's a coven out there that can control that many hunters, I don't see why we can't figure out something like that too. We should be able to create a spell that can stop the hunters from their thirst to kill. There must be a way," Margo responds.

"Enough witch-talk for the rest of the drive, girls. This short car ride is our only free time from witch-stuff today. Everything else today is going to be witch-related and a little crazy. Let's enjoy this free moment, shall we?"

"So, now are you going to tell us where we're going?" Margo asks wistfully, already flipping her mood.

"Nope."

"Boo," I respond playfully, kicking the back of his seat.

Callen smiles at me in the mirror. He messes with his music folder on the large touch screen. After making his selection, he pumps the volume up and rolls the windows down.

I lean forward. "I didn't take you as an Interrupters fan," I shout over the ska music blaring from the speakers.

"I could say the same to you," he laughs.

"Touché."

"Did you know the lead singer and the guitarist are married?" he asks.

"I haven't been living under a rock." I laugh. "You have better taste in music than I thought you'd have."

A full, pleased grin slowly spreads across his face. We catch eyes in the mirror again, and I swear he's blushing, which causes me to blush. My face is now beaming hot red, and my insides are tingling.

Margo eyes me curiously, and I know it's time to cool it down with Callen. I didn't expect to have so much in common with him. We've connected on a spiritual level, caffeinated beverages, and now music.

Just friends.

That's all.

"I have no clue who this is," Tahlia says, her voice drowning in the angsty but upbeat music.

"I'm not sure I know them either, but I'm digging it," Margo adds, letting the music invade her body as she dances in her seat.

Callen and I burst into the chorus of "Take Back the Power," singing loudly with the windows rolled down and the sun shining through the sunroof, warming my skin.

Callen weaves through the backroads, leaving East Gate in the rear window. I don't question where we're going and why we're leaving town because for a split second, I don't care. I'm attempting to enjoy the ride, as Callen suggested. Mile after country road mile, my stress melts away. For a moment, I'm a typical high schooler hanging out with my friends—my real friends.

But then my stomach twists as we pull into a town slightly smaller than ours, making me remember that I'm a witch, and we're a coven with a huge burden on our shoulders. At least I got a few moments of freedom before opening the doors of madness again.

Callen slowly yanks the car off the road, parking in front of an old, run-down block of shops. We walk to the far end of the street in silence. The last shop on the right is an old, rusty-colored, brick building with no street-facing windows, only a narrow-framed door. The tiny sign above the entryway reads, *Invoke Awakenings.*

"This is your surprise," Callen says, beaming.

Tahlia turns her nose upward. "I'm confused."

"We need supplies. If we're going to do this witch thing right, we need to be prepared," Callen responds.

"How do you know so much, brother of mine?" she taunts.

"I've been studying ever since I found out I was different. I decided to harness my powers and make them useful. So, yes, I know some stuff."

"Why couldn't we have gone to that oddities shop downtown? I'm sure they have the same things," Tahlia asks.

"The kind of things we're looking for can't be found there. Trust me, this store is special. It's one of a kind. Plus, we don't know people here, and the chances of us running into anyone are very slim. Remember, we need to keep a low profile in East Gate."

"This could be fun," Margo says gleefully.

"So, what's on our list?" I ask.

"First, a proper athame. No more kitchen knives, you got it?"

"Yes," we respond in unison.

"Second, a book of shadows—a place where we can record our own spells and rituals."

I kick at the ground below, nervous to ask my next question. "Speaking of that. You know how Isobel and her coven were named The Wives of Salem Coven? I think we should have a name too. You know, to make us more official and stuff. What do you think of The Witches of East Gate Coven?" I don't know why, but I feel silly after the words leave my mouth. I carefully eye each of my coven mates for their reaction.

Margo's eyes light up. "Oh, I love it. It's perfect."

"I like it too," Tahlia says.

"Well, then, it's settled. We have a name," Callen responds. "Our High Priestess, Izzy Beswick, has completed her first duty by naming our coven." His words are slightly jokey, but still, my insides tingle with acceptance.

"You guys, it's really happening," I respond, grinning with excitement. "So, what else is on our list? Anything in particular we should be looking for?"

"I'll get the important items. I want you girls to gather anything that calls to you. And don't worry about the money. This is my treat." His eyes fall to me and Margo, making me feel like a charity case.

It's coming from a good place, and he means well, so I'm grateful for his generosity.

"It's important that we do things properly from this point on." Callen holds the door open for us.

"Agreed. No more mistakes," Margo says, sliding past Callen.

Inside the store smells exactly like I'd expect. Patchouli oil and a mix of incense invade my senses, nearly making my eyes water.

Callen bends down and grabs four wicker baskets and hands them out. Margo and Tahlia eagerly take off, leaving me alone with Callen, but I'm happy with that. He's been my teacher so far, so I'm excited to wander around with him and see what he chooses for us.

The store is larger than I imagined from the outside. It's narrow and very long with the cash register near the back.

I've yet to see the shop clerk, but that's OK. The fewer interactions, the better.

The first row of dusty shelves houses a multitude of beautiful raw crystals. Most I don't know the names for, but I know an amethyst when I see one. One in particular catches my eye; it's on the smaller side, showing several shades of purple and layered with imperfections. It's rather pretty, but I set it back and continue to follow Callen around the store. He grabs a handful of odd shaped sticks, labeled palo santo, and places them in his basket. Then proceeds to tuck several bundles of white sage and a large seashell next to the sticks. I'm hoping he tells me what their uses are later.

"Put these in your basket." He hands me a group of white candles. "Remember, white is for protection."

Goosebumps quilt my body, and a sick feeling of recklessness creeps over me. "I remember. I imagined white last night, just like you said, but we didn't have protection candles when we did my dad's spell. Did we make a mistake?"

"It's fine; these only add to the intensity of the spell," Callen reassures me.

Somehow, I do feel better. Well, slightly less worried.

He drops a few more candles in my basket. "The black is for absorbing negative energy. The green is for healing, just in case."

Callen plucks a pink candle from the shelf and drops it into his basket without explanation. I want to ask him about it, but I don't. Instead, I follow him to a library-style shelf of thick, diary-like books.

"You should pick our book of shadows," Callen suggests.

I run my fingers over the spines, trying to stir up my intuition, letting the book call to me. I close my eyes and run my hand back in the other direction. A slight burst of movement causes me to pause and shift my eyes open. To a wandering eye, this movement isn't noticeable, but I experienced the tiny shift, and I know this is the one.

I tug on the thick, black leather spine, yanking it from its burrowed home on the shelf. It's heavy, just like the one in my bag. I caress the cover, feeling good about my intuitive decision.

"I choose this one," I say confidently, handing it to Callen for final approval.

He nods and smiles as he inspects my choice. "Wood binding, genuine leather, antique style with rustic looking pages. You did well, Beswick."

I waggle my fingers. "Intuitive magic."

He proudly grins, placing the heavy book alongside the other items in his wicker basket.

We continue to wander around, meeting the girls in front of a glass counter where Margo is carefully eyeing the items inside.

"I found our athame. It's this one." Margo points to a beautiful stainless-steel knife with a black handle. The base of the blade resembles a Celtic cross with a red design weaved over black plating. A simple silver emblem of the tree of life is welded into the middle of the design.

"It's perfect." I eye the object, knowing it must have spoken to Margo the same way the book chose me.

Margo flags down an employee. "I would like this athame, please, sir."

A slender man grabs a set of keys from the wall behind him. He intensely eyes Margo before carefully taking the item out of the case.

Is he checking her out? What a perv. He's at least twenty years older than us.

The man places the knife on a black piece of cloth for us to view.

"Looks great, we'll take it," Callen says.

But the man doesn't look at him. Instead, his honey-colored eyes continue to creepily wander across Margo's exposed skin and down into her cleavage.

I can sense Margo getting nervous.

I part my mouth, gearing up to say something—to stop him from staring, but the man speaks first.

"That's an interesting necklace, young lady. Where did you get it?"

I let out a sigh of relief when he says *necklace*. I glance at Margo, who's wearing the same piece of jewelry she's worn since the day I met her. It's the large purple and black antique-looking pendant necklace. I've never thought to ask Margo where she got it. It's stunning, but to me, it's part of her style. I don't think twice when I see it, like Tahlia wearing a lot of black, or Jessa dressing posh; it's just their looks.

Margo places her hand over the pendant, and a vibration radiates from her. It's strange.

"It's a family heirloom," she responds, keeping her hand firmly covering the necklace.

"It's special. You should take good care of it," the man

says, sliding our athame into a sheath. "I'll have this waiting for you at the register."

I wait for the clerk to walk away before responding, "Um, that was strange."

"I know, right," Margo responds, curling her lips downward, while anxiously stroking the necklace.

"Who did your necklace belong to?" I ask.

"I'm not sure. I've just been told it's a family heirloom."

"Well, as the man said, it's special and you should take good care of it," Callen mocks.

"I have a couple more things I want to look at," Tahlia says, pulling Margo with her. "Meet you at the register in a bit."

Callen and I weave through the long aisles, searching for more necessities. He adds a chalice, a white container of salt, a black bowl, and some blue candles to our growing pile, then we continue to the rear of the store. A piece of purple lightweight fabric dangles over a narrow opening in the far backside of the store. With each stir of movement, it flutters, exposing a long table and a slender woman with long black hair. She doesn't call to me out loud, but I sense she wants to see me. With little thought, I pull the fabric back.

The woman with dazzling emerald eyes and hair darker than night invites us to take a seat at her table, gesturing with her hands.

"A reading?" she asks.

Callen stares quizzically at me.

I ignore his concerns and respond, "Yes."

She carefully chooses a deck of cards, pulling a beautiful midnight-blue deck embellished with silver stars.

"Izzy, are you sure you want to do this?" Callen whispers.

I grin and the woman continues by shuffling the deck several times. She pulls a card with her left hand and places it face down in front of me, then does the same with two more cards.

"Your past, present, and future," she says, gliding her hand over her beautiful cards.

With the same hand, she flips the first card. "Your past. The Fool and it's reversed. Irresponsibility and foolishness led you on your path, making you leap before looking, but you started a journey, nonetheless." Her blazing emerald eyes meet mine.

I feel compelled to agree. This card could represent our move to East Gate or diving headfirst into magic without knowing much, but it seems it's correct.

I stir in my seat as I study the gorgeous card. It's a man with a knapsack who's about to blindly step off a cliff. The guy appears blissfully happy and unaware of his fate, but seems all right with his decision. At a second glance, the card makes me queasy. A cliff—Sondra—Anna. I'm reading too much into it. I release a long breath, calming my nerves that are now on edge.

The woman clears her throat, bringing me back to the room.

"Next is your present." She flips the card. "Hmm, the Tower card."

I don't like the way she said that.

My gaze falls to the newly turned up card—my present. The image sends a rush of heat through my limbs. The card depicts a horrid sight, a burning tower atop a mountain that's being struck with lightning. There are two people leaping headfirst from the burning tower's windows. It screams chaos and destruction.

"You've had some sudden changes, I suspect?"

I nod.

"Do you feel like your world is falling apart? Maybe you went so far down the wrong path, you don't feel there's a way out now. Perhaps something big just happened?"

Tears fall from my eyes as I shake my head.

"Dear, it's OK to ask for help. You're not on your journey alone." She motions to Callen.

That's right, I have my coven to keep me safe.

"Your final card—your future." She slowly flips the card, revealing a person who appears ready for battle. "Seven of wands."

She pulls in an attentive breath. "Wands are associated with fire and unpredictability, but also strength and determination."

An unease settles over me as it seems she's describing me and not the card.

I'm suddenly ready for this reading to end, but my legs don't move. My body's stiff in my seat.

"Are you fighting off others? Preparing for a competition in your future? Protecting what's yours? Either way, you need to stand up for what you believe is right."

How about protecting myself from hunters and dead relatives?

The stranger sitting across from me reaches over the table and places her hand on mine. My fire rages through her touch, and I sense she knows what I am.

Her grin fades as a wave of terror washes over her

emerald eyes. "You have a dark spirit around you, girl. There is something attached to your dark shadow." The woman pulls her arm away with haste and stands alert.

"I can't help you anymore. Please leave."

CHAPTER 15
YOU LIED

I dash out of the building, leaving my basket, the sounds of my friend's voices fading behind me. I keep running until I'm next to the car, my chest pounding, and my breath coming out heavy and labored with wheezes. I hurl forward, trying to control my breathing, but it doesn't help. I'm dying for a sip of water, but the car is locked. I slump down onto the curb in defeat and tuck my head between my legs, letting my hair dangle all around me.

Just breathe, Izzy.

"What the heck happened?" Margo asks, swinging a bag from her hand. "I saw you take off, but Callen told us to give you a moment. Are you all right?"

"That woman in there gave me a tarot reading. When it was over, she touched me and told me I have a dark spirit around me, then told me to leave. She said I had something attached to my dark shadow, whatever the hell that means. Margo, it was truly disturbing."

"Oh dang, Izzy. That's freaky. I'm sorry I wasn't in there with you. I would have given that lady a piece of my mind.

But sweetie, I wouldn't put too much stock into what she said. She might have just been playing with you."

"I don't know, Margo. She seemed legit."

"Hey, shake it off. We're going to see your lover boy now. Cheer up."

The thought of seeing Riley does make me happy. I should have been with him this whole time, instead of on some surprise outing with Callen. We didn't do anything to move the needle toward breaking the curse. All I learned is that I have a dark passenger riding shotgun that the tarot lady can see, but I can't.

"Don't think about it anymore," Margo says, nudging my foot.

An electric surge of energy churns around us, pulling our attention to the Latham-Hart siblings sprinting toward us in a panic.

"We've got to go now! Izzy, there's been an accident," Tahlia cries.

I'm staring at her, trying to comprehend what she's said, but her words don't make sense. "An accident?"

"Your dad, Izzy. He's in the hospital," she explains.

Lightheadedness creeps over me, and the ground spins, making me faint. "No, that can't be." I attempt to stand but fall back onto the curb.

Their words twist through my head—Dad—hospital. It's not possible.

"Callen, you said we protected him. How can my dad be in the hospital?"

"What did you two do?" Tahlia questions.

"Last night, we performed a protection spell to keep Steven safe from Anna, just in case."

"You did what? You two were together last night?" Tahlia says, shocked.

"Can we please go? I'll explain later. We aren't accomplishing anything by making a scene here," Callen pleads.

"Is my dad OK? Please tell me," I beg.

"We don't know for sure," Tahlia responds softly. "We just need to go."

Callen's hands grip my arms, but I don't budge.

"Izzy, get in the car. We need to go now." He tightens his grasp on me.

My breath falters as I allow Callen to help me upright. "You told me to trust you, and I did. You lied to me."

Heavy tears snake down my hot skin, stirring up my anger inside. Without thinking, I shove Callen into the car, thrashing my hands wildly at him. I push my palms deep into his chest, wanting him to feel my pain.

He grabs both my wrists with one hand and pulls me tightly against his torso. A jolt of vibration surges through our bodies.

"Calm breaths, Izzy. It's going to be OK." His words burn hot against my skin, but they have a calming effect on me, like a spell.

The air grows dense around us, blocking out all other sounds, including my friends. I know they're speaking, but I can't make out their words.

Each time Callen's chest inflates, mine deflates, as if we're breathing as one.

His lips press against the top of my head. "Izzy, you have to believe me. I thought he'd be safe. I would never do anything to hurt you. I need you to get in the car, so we can go to the hospital."

My body gives way and obeys his direction as he guides me into my seat. He pulls the seatbelt over me, securing me.

The thud of the three remaining doors securing into place pulls me away from my calming trance as the invasion of questions flicker through the air.

I don't move. I don't respond.

The drive is a blur as we roar through the countryside, taking the road faster than the speed limit permits. I hear bits and pieces of Callen explaining our spell and our evening spent together. Margo and Tahlia chime in with gasps and sudden movements of exasperation.

I messed up.

I should have called Riley last night.

Or maybe I should have let Callen call his parents.

But now it's too late.

My dad is in trouble, and it's all my fault.

I close my eyes, pressing my palms deep into the sockets to calm the madness overtaking my brain.

I can't lose him.

I can't lose my dad.

CHAPTER 16
HELP ME

When we arrive at the hospital, Barrett, Riley, and Jessa are frantically pacing the sidewalk by the emergency entrance. The shrill wail of sirens echoes in the distance, making my stomach flip. How can my dad be here? He was fine this morning when I left him. I knew I should have gone home to check on him.

Trust me, Callen said.

Ugh, I could spit on Callen's trust right about now.

From the trio, Riley looks our way first. My pace quickens when our eyes lock.

"Izzy," he yells, hastening his steps to greet me. He encircles both arms around me until he's fully holding me in an affectionate embrace.

I pull away just enough to peer up at his watery blue eyes. "Where's my dad?"

He stumbles for his words with tears stifling his voice. "Izzy, it's not good."

"Where is he? Where is my dad?" I plead.

"I'm not sure. Jessa and I just got here."

"Together?"

"Yes, we were at the Latham-Hart house waiting for you guys when Barrett called home to tell Bree what happened. We came as fast as we could."

Barrett approaches with his usual studiousness, but this time, I'm cautioned by the sea of tears that veil his shadowy eyes.

"He's with a team of specialists right now," Barrett says.

"Specialists?" I choke out the word like it's caught in my throat.

Barrett gives me a sympathetic stare. "They wouldn't tell me anything more since I'm not family. But you're here now. So, let's go get some answers."

I twist from Riley's embrace and dash through the sliding emergency entrance. I don't pay attention to who's behind me, but when I stop at the reception desk and see the line of people waiting, I turn to see everyone came after me, except for Callen. *Where did he go?*

"The line isn't moving," I say to anyone who's listening.

"It will be your turn soon," Barrett reassures me.

He turns to face my group of friends, who are obstructing the entryway. "Why don't you guys all take a seat while I wait with Izzy up here?"

Riley looks at me warily, searching for my approval to leave my side. I nod and he joins my friends, who are already heading toward the waiting area.

"How did you know to come here?" I ask Barrett.

He inhales deeply through his nose and exhales. "I was at your house, trying to keep an eye on our situation."

I give a slight nod, understanding that he's referring to Anna.

"That's when I saw your dad through the back door in

your kitchen. He was having a hard time breathing. I made up some excuse as to why I was there. I tried to help him, but he kept getting worse. That's when I called 911."

"Where was Anna?"

"I never saw her. I don't think she was there."

The line inches forward.

"Why didn't you heal him?"

His eyes grow confused.

In a hushed voice, I clarify, "I saw you heal Anna's wound in the forest." I gasp at the reality of my words because if what I'm saying is true . . .

"Oh, my goodness. It's all your fault. You healed her too much, and she came back." I take a shy step away from my friend's father.

"Izzy, it's not like that." Barrett reaches out, but he drops his hand before it reaches me. "You're confused."

"Then what did I see?"

"I glamoured the wound. I can't heal people, Izzy. I'm not that strong. Glamour is a—"

"I know what glamouring is." I cut him off.

"Next," a nasally voice calls from behind the receptionist desk.

We slowly inch forward, getting closer to my answers, but still not close enough.

"I can't heal people, and I most certainly can't bring people back from the dead," he whispers.

I continue in my hushed voice, but by the looks of the distraught people around us, I doubt that what I'm saying is more important than their concerns right now.

"Do you think Anna did something to my dad?"

"I wish I knew, Izzy. It might not be related to Anna at all."

"But no matter what, we need to find out how she came back."

"Agreed, and that's what I was trying to do when . . ." His words trail off.

"Next."

Finally.

"My dad . . . Steven Beswick. Where is he?" I say, panicked, pushing my way around Barrett.

I watch as the woman slowly pecks his name on her keyboard, one finger at a time.

Could you be any slower?

In addition to her maddeningly slow typing skills, she keeps pausing to push her glasses that have fallen down her sweaty nose.

Seriously.

"Steven Beswick. Have you found him?" I impatiently ask, leaning over the counter as she proceeds to look through a mess of files around her desk.

"Are you a family member?" She pushes her glasses up again.

"Yes, I'm his daughter." I slide my driver's license under her nose to hurry the process along.

"Miss Beswick, your father is with a specialist right now. The doctor will come find you if you want to take a seat in the waiting area." She gestures to the door behind us.

"I already knew all of that. Can you tell me why he was admitted?"

She pecks at the keyboard again, then looks up with her eyes peeking over her glasses. "Respiratory distress."

"What does that mean?"

"You'll have to wait to speak with the doctor. I'm just a receptionist, ma'am. I'll let the doctor know to find you in the waiting room when he's done with the patient."

"He's not a patient. He's a person. He's my father."

I let out an exasperated huff instead of reaching over the counter to slug her for her lack of empathy.

"Respiratory distress? What is that?" I ask Barrett.

"I'm not certain, but your dad was having a hard time breathing. It's like his lungs couldn't keep up," Barrett responds.

"My dad is healthy. This doesn't make sense."

"These kinds of things happen, Izzy. Even to the healthiest people."

I know he's right, but I can't help but think Anna did this to him. And where is she now?

My friends eagerly gather around us when we enter the waiting room, their faces guarded with worry.

"What did they say?" Tahlia asks.

"Can you see him?" Jessa and Margo's voices blend together in a single question.

I drop into the first available seat. "No, he's still with the specialist. They won't tell me anything."

"Izzy, he's going to be fine. I know it," Margo reassures me.

But that's what people are supposed to say. That's what people said about my mom.

Then she died.

The cloying scent of antiseptics and cheap soap lingering in the air serves as a constant reminder that death is happening all over this hospital, and there isn't anything I can do about it.

I couldn't do anything to help my mom, and I can't do anything to help my dad. I'm useless.

My friends grow silent as the time ticks by.

Waiting. Waiting. Waiting.

When a gray-haired man with tired eyes wearing a long white lab coat enters the room, I jolt to his attention. "Steven Beswick? Are you his doctor?"

"His daughter, I presume," he responds, standing with perfect posture and folded hands.

"Yes, that's me. I'm Izzy. My dad, Steven Beswick, is he OK?"

"Would you prefer to chat in private, Miss Beswick?" he queries, glaring at my gaggle of companions who are eagerly eyeing him from behind me.

I glance at my friends, then back at the doctor. "Whatever you need to say, you can say it in front of my friends, Doctor."

"Alright, Miss Beswick. Do you know if your dad has come into contact with hemlock?"

"Wh-what's that?" I stutter.

"It's a poisonous plant that has toxic compounds called alkaloids, which were found in your father's system. Our woods are littered with hemlock if you venture out far enough. It's sad to say, but this isn't my first time dealing with this plant. He's lucky someone called 911, or he might have died."

His words rattle me. "I don't know. I mean, last night he said he was out back looking for me when I didn't come home right away."

"Is it a wooded area?"

"Yes."

"He may have stumbled upon some. It's poisonous to the touch." He pinches his lips together tightly before continuing. "But it also seems he may have ingested some of it, which isn't as common."

"That doesn't make sense. Why would he eat a plant?" I feel myself getting defensive.

"Maybe when he wakes up, he can tell us. But for right now, we have him stable and on a ventilator. We'll continue to flush his system. His kidneys are showing signs of distress as well. This is going to be hard to hear, but if you have any close relatives, I would get them on the phone. He may need a kidney transplant at some point, and it's always easier when you're prepared."

"A kidney transplant?"

"It might not come down to it, but it's best to get ahead of these kinds of things, instead of behind."

"Can I see him?"

"Yes, but it will need to be a quick visit. He's in the intensive care unit. Room B."

Intensive care. Ventilator. Kidney failure. Hemlock. All the doctor's words spin around me, making me nauseous.

"Are you sure you're up to seeing your dad like that?" Riley asks, walking me to the elevator.

"I have to. He's my dad, and he's all alone."

"I wish I could go with you."

"Me too."

He smiles as the elevator door opens. I walk in, turn

around, and as the door is closing, Riley's eyes shift to a darker blue. He pulls away, leaving me with a disturbed feeling that things are about to change.

In Dad's room, he's hooked up to several machines, not just the ventilator that the doctor said. I feel lied to about his condition. It appears even worse than he described. I pull a chair close to his bed and weave my fingers into his. His hands are icy but growing warmer from my touch.

"Dad, it's me, Izzy. I'm not sure if you can hear me, but I'm here. They won't let me stay long. I don't know how this happened to you, but don't worry, I'm going to figure it out. I'm so sorry I wasn't home."

Heavy tears rush from my eyes, making me pull away from Dad to reach for a tissue. As I twist back around, I feel lightheaded again. Suddenly, the air swirls around me, then stops. The loose piece of hair dangling out of place is slowly tucked behind my ear. The sensation causes fire to roar through my entire body, heating every cell inside me. The movement was soft and endearing, but there's something strange and unnerving about it.

"Anna? Isobel? Are you with me again?" I softly whisper, letting more tears flow down my cheeks.

"Help me," a faint, strained voice calls out.

CHAPTER 17
DEAD PEOPLE CAN TALK

"Help. Me. Izzy," the faint, wary voice cries, sending another round of flames through my body.

I gaze at my dad, lying lifeless in his hospital bed, but it isn't Dad's voice I hear; it's a woman's voice.

It's Anna's.

"How?" I question the thin air around me.

No response.

"Anna?" I call out.

Nothing.

A white pair of shoes exposes themselves in the cracked doorway, and I know I'm not alone anymore. A round-framed nurse with frizzy red hair pushes the door wide open.

"Sweetie, intensive care visiting hours are over. I'm afraid it's time to go."

"No, I barely got to see him."

She steps further into the room. "I know, sweetie, but there's not much you can do for him right now. He knows you want to be here." Her voice is kind, making me feel bad for what I'm about to ask next.

"Are you sure I can't stay? I won't tell anyone you let me."

She frowns at my attempt. "I'm afraid rules are rules. You can come back tomorrow."

I want to keep fighting her, but it's useless. I lean in and give Dad a kiss on the cheek. "I'll be back tomorrow. Please don't leave me, Dad. I need you. I love you."

"Anna?" I softly question as I walk out of the room. Once again, nothing.

Back in the waiting room, Riley and Barrett are the only ones there. "Where did everyone go?"

"I had Callen take everyone back to our house."

Callen, he was still here. He didn't leave me.

"We still have a lot of things to discuss tonight. Izzy, you'll be staying with us. I can't in good conscience let you stay alone tonight with Anna out there somewhere. I'll follow the two of you to your house so you can pack a bag, then we must hurry and get back to my house. Everyone is waiting. How's your dad?"

"Hooked up to tubes. I honestly don't know." I hang my head and follow the guys to the parking lot, keeping my Anna experience to myself.

Riley and I get into his car, and we follow Barrett to my house.

"This is the first time I've been in your car."

"It's nothing special," Riley responds.

He's right. It's nothing special. It's a gray base model, Honda sedan, that at a quick glance, has over one-hundred thousand miles. A definite downgrade from my other friend's vehicles, yet I find comfort in it. Riley's like me.

"I'm so sorry about your dad. Do you want to talk about it some more?"

"I'd rather not. I just want to be with you in this moment. We may not get many more. I can't keep losing people, Riley. My heart can't take it."

His fingers glide through his floppy, soft brown hair as his face scrunches up in a frown. "I bet you wish you didn't move to East Gate."

I twist in my seat to face him better. I put my hand on top of his, which is now on the gear shifter. "Silly as it sounds, but before the hospital tonight, I wouldn't have agreed with that. Now I'm questioning everything. But don't think for a second that I'm regretting you."

"You might change your mind on that in a couple of days."

"Hey, there's still hope."

"Let's just say I'm running out of what little hope I had after being with hunters all day."

"Why? What happened?" I rub his hand.

"I spent most of my time with Bree and a bit of it with my father in that creepy basement. It was hard seeing him in that cage again, Izzy. He begged me to let him go. I'm not going to lie to you, I thought about it. I thought that maybe he could run and start over, but then I saw your face and the image of him hovering over you with that knife. This whole thing is really messing with me." A single tear falls from his eye. "On one hand, he's my dad, but on the other, he's a murderer. I have to accept that he's not the man I thought he was my whole life." He wipes away the lone tear, leaving a wet streak across his cheek. "What if I end up in a cage just like him because I can't control myself? Promise me that if I ever try to hurt you, you'll lock me up and throw away the key. It's what I'll deserve."

"I'm not going to let that happen, Riley." I clasp his hand tightly, hoping my embrace calms him.

"Izzy, I'm not sure how much longer it's safe for us to be alone together."

"Hey, let's take this one hour at a time. Right now, we're fine." I say the words, but I'm not sure how much truth there is to them. I might be feeling overly perceptive, but I sense a slight shift around him.

"You know, I think my dad enjoys being a hunter. He'd be pissed if we took that away from him. Even Bree, I think she enjoys the power it gives her. Being a hunter, it makes her feel special—superior to others even. It's kind of sick. She acts all self-righteous, but deep down, if it came to it, I don't think she could give it up."

"You'd think she'd want to break the curse. It's been a burden to her since she turned eighteen, keeping her from freely being around her husband and son and potentially her daughter."

"You'd think." Riley frowns. "Maybe you shouldn't talk about our plan to break the curse around her. Just in case I'm right about Bree."

"OK. Make sure the others know that too. We've probably already said too much," I add.

"We need to be careful around everyone."

"Riley, it's going to be OK. We'll find a way if that's what you truly want. Then we'll make it happen."

"Of course, it's what I want," he snaps.

I'm taken aback by his little outburst, but I let it go because he's stressed. Time isn't on our side.

"If a witch placed the curse, then a witch can break the curse. Right?" My words sliver on the edge of hope.

"I hope you're right. That Elizabeth Crowley is some w-i-t-c-h." Witch rolls off his tongue like a bad word.

I don't respond in fear of saying the wrong thing. His taste for my kind is growing more unpleasant by the second.

"Seriously, I get that she was pissed that her friends ditched her, but to continually punish them is just sick. Isn't witchcraft about karma?" Riley huffs.

"Yes, I think so. What you put out there, you get back," I respond.

"Well, I guess she got death, but she chose that for herself. So, is it really punishment?" Riley says, with a hint of infuriation in his voice.

"I suppose not, but maybe she's getting her just reward somewhere else."

"Like hell?"

"Or maybe another realm." My words slip.

I've only told Callen about that experience. I'm not sure how much I should tell Riley, especially if he's changing. It could put the other witches at risk.

I want to trust him, but I need to have my guard up. This is even more of a reason to find a way to break the curse. But I might need his help with the Anna thing, so I guess he'll eventually find out.

"Another realm?" He curiously questions as he takes the

last right and begins the ascent up the hill to my house.

"I don't know for certain, but I think it's a place where witches cross through or live in limbo or something. I'm not entirely sure, but there's a place for them. I've been there. It's not heaven or hell. It's just there."

Riley eyes me curiously.

"You don't believe me?"

"No, of course I do."

"I want to tell you something."

"You can tell me." He squeezes my hand, and it frenzies with fire.

Listen to your gift, Izzy.

He shakes my hand, nudging me to continue.

Hello, fire.

Are you listening?

What are you telling me?

I can't read your signals.

Ah, fuck it.

"I think Anna had something to do with my dad." The words roll hot and fast off my tongue. "I mean, why would he eat hemlock? That doesn't make sense. He must have been fed it—by Anna or whatever she is. She poisoned him," I add.

"Why would she poison her own son?"

"Right, which brings me to my next thing. Anna spoke to me in the hospital."

"Wait. She was there?"

"Well, no. Not in a physical form. But I heard her voice. I think there's something wrong. I think she needs help."

"Why would you want to help the woman who poisoned your dad?"

"That's the thing. I don't think the woman that poisoned my dad and the woman that called to me are the same person. I don't think the Anna we all saw this morning is the real Anna. I know that sounds insane. I think the real Anna died because we all witnessed it, but her soul is somehow trapped in that other realm. I know that makes zero sense, yet it's the only thing that makes sense." I uncomfortably shift in my seat, feeling insecure over my thoughts.

"I think I get what you're saying."

"She wants me to help her, and I think that's what I'm supposed to do."

Riley pulls the car off the street, parking directly behind Barrett's SUV.

"So, what do you propose we do then?" he asks.

"I don't know, but I feel the answer will come to us." I push open my door and slide my leg out, but turn back toward him. "Will you come in with me?"

"Of course. I wasn't planning on letting you go in alone," he sweetly responds like the Riley I know, already pulling the key from the ignition.

Barrett greets us on the sidewalk. "I'm going to walk the perimeter, but the house looks the same as when I left. Holler if you need me."

He's gone before I have time to beg him to come in with us.

***

In my bedroom, I toss a random assortment of clothing items into a bag, mindlessly piecing together a day's worth of clothing. I quickly shove my toiletries into a smaller bag that fits into my larger bag. Before leaving, I wait until Riley isn't looking, and I double check that my knife is where I left it last night.

Nothing looks out of place. Good.

I secure both of my bags over my body: the one with the diary and spell book and my overnight bag.

"Hey, before we head downstairs—" Riley breaks mid-sentence, taking me by the hand, swinging me around to meet his face. His eyes flicker between smokey dark blue and dusty light blue in the iridescent lighting.

He grins and pulls me closer. "I doubt we'll get much alone time tonight."

I giggle, falling into his embrace, letting his lips greet mine. I close my eyes and let him kiss me. When my eyes part open, I'm mystified by the shift in eye color yet again. It's not the lighting. His body is changing. His eyes swirl into a midnight blue. The color twinkles, making him cuter than before, if that's even possible.

His grin twists mischievously into a smirk as he moves back in, letting his lips aggressively press against mine. It's unlike any kiss I've ever felt, making me both eager to continue but frightened, wanting to pull away.

Izzy, something isn't right. You need to get away.

But I don't listen to my brain elbowing me to run.

Instead, I lean into his kiss, which is fierce and sexy, making me feel desired for the first time in my life. My body goes limp in his arms, allowing him to take control.

Izzy, you're being careless.

I ignore my warning, bringing my hand up to his hair, letting my fingers run through his brown locks.

"I want you, Izzy," he says, kissing my neck.

My body tingles from his words.

"Riley," I softly call out.

I drop my arm to his biceps, which are bulging out of his tight T-shirt. The edge of his tattoo is peeking out, taunting me, reminding me of what he is—a hunter.

My body quivers as I relish in his yearning for me, but reality is punching harder and winning the battle.

"We should go. Barrett's waiting," I say, pulling away.

He doesn't listen, instead Riley yanks me closer and kisses me more intensely, so hard it hurts. The roughness of his force burns my lips.

I try to yank away, but he doesn't stop.

"Riley, you're hurting me," I attempt to say through pressed lips.

This is no longer sexy; it's chilling. The heat that swarms through me cools with every movement.

I know what it's telling me.

I need to run.

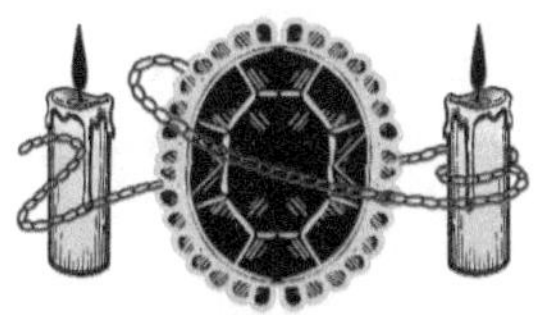

CHAPTER 18
SEXY TIME IS OVER

I twist my body, trying to wiggle from Riley's tight hold on me.

"Please, stop," I plead.

My body is out of sync with his as our hearts pump against our pressed chests, his heart beating rapidly, almost unhuman like.

"Riley?"

"Please, Riley. You need to stop. This isn't you. Sexy time is over."

He pivots with me in his arms and shoves me against the wall. His breath grows into an unruly pant, becoming erratic and abnormal.

"Riley. What's going on?"

"Witch," he hisses, pinning me against the wall.

Hot tears release from my eyes, burning as they pour down my face. "It's happening, Riley. You don't hate me. I'm your girlfriend. We've known each other forever. We were friends. This isn't you." My words dance through the air without registering with him.

"Riley, it's not time. We still have three more days. You can't change—no—this can't be it."

His breath intensifies, exaggerating with each intake, making me even more nervous.

"Babe, it's me. Listen to me—to my words. Calm your breath. It's going to be OK. I'm not mad at you."

His darkened eyes slowly spiral into a lighter version of blue.

"I know it's soon, but I love you. I've loved you since we were kids."

His eyes flicker with hope, shifting back to their normal baby blue color that I love so much. His breath retreats to a slower pace.

"You lo—" His words are abruptly silenced as the door swings open into us, knocking Riley off his balance, but not quite enough to free me from his hold.

"Izzy! Izzy, are you OK?" Callen cries out, nearly out of breath, panting as he dashes into the room. He spins around, and his eyes grow wild when he sees me pinned in place by my boyfriend.

"Callen," I whimper. "What are you doing here?"

"Saving you from him—the hunter," Callen scoffs, his voice harsh and cold as he glowers at Riley.

"Callen, I had it under control," I boldly declare.

"By the looks of it, you didn't."

Riley shakes his head vigorously as if he's emerging from a trance. "What happened?"

"You were going to hurt her," Callen sneers, pulling on my arm.

"Riley, it's OK. You didn't hurt me."

I gently rub his arm. His entire body is tense.

Callen continues to pull me out of harm's way, freely tossing me near my bed. He shoves Riley in the shoulder, pushing him against the wall. He pulls his fist back and thrusts it past Riley's face, hitting the wall, while making his point very clear.

"If you harm one hair on that girl's head—Riley Hawkins, I will kill you."

"No. I would never hurt her. Izzy, I wasn't going to hurt you, right?" His stammering words cause a feeling of nausea to wash over me.

I nervously avert my gaze to the ground. "I'm not sure, Riley."

One fat tear wells in Riley's eye, covering his baby blue color like a watery veil. He blinks and it flushes down his handsome face, making me feel conflicted. I want to run to him and tell him it's OK, but next time, it might not be.

"Riley, I think your wires got crossed. I think the intention started off in the right place, but the hunter side started to sneak in, and it took things to an intense level. I know you didn't mean to hurt me, but I don't think it's good for us to be alone until we break the curse."

"And as for you—" I walk over to Callen and slug him in the arm. "You keep messing things up. My dad wouldn't be in the hospital if it weren't for you and your dumb spell idea. And I did have this under control." I slug him again.

"Geez, Beswick. I'm just trying to help."

"Why do you care so much?" Riley asks. "You always

seem to be around these days." His lip curls into a menacing sneer, baring his perfectly straight teeth.

"She's a bloodline witch, and I have to keep her safe." Callen responds.

I know that's not the only reason, but I don't entertain the idea for too long because he could be listening to my thoughts.

"Barrett's waiting for us. We need to go," I inform the hunter and the witch standing in my bedroom.

"Izzy, you're riding with me," Callen instructs.

"No, I'm riding with Barrett," I confidently say, marching out of my bedroom, leaving both boys trailing behind.

"How did you know to come here? How did you know she was in trouble?" Riley softly asks Callen, his words muddled in confusion and sadness.

"We're connected," Callen replies.

I don't dare turn around because I'm certain Riley's face will be full of dejection, and it will break my heart.

Riley and I are supposed to be connected. We're supposed to be the kindred spirits.

I do love him, though.

I meant what I said.

CHAPTER 19
COMMITTED NO CRIME

At the Latham-Hart house, Bree is dishing up pizza from several open pizza boxes when the four of us arrive. My mouth waters as the smell of delicious greasiness wafts through the air. As I've recently learned, there's always room for comfort food, especially during a crisis.

When I approach the long, rectangular, wooden kitchen table, Jessa, Margo, and Tahlia are deep in conversation. I assume they've resolved their issues from earlier today. Tragedy has a way of doing that.

"Finally," Jessa huffs as I get closer, seemingly back to her old self.

The other girls pause, their eyes filling with sorrow.

"Sorry, we had to swing by my house, so I could grab an overnight bag." I flash the bag dangling along my side.

"You're spending the night too?" Margo gleefully asks.

"Yup."

"Good. So are we." Margo nods to Jessa.

"Aren't your parents going to start noticing you girls never go home? You're always here," Bree asks.

"Nope," Jessa says, sliding a thin piece of plain cheese pizza into her mouth.

"The food's too good here. Why would we ever want to leave?" Margo responds, with a teasing smile. "What about you, Riley? Are you staying here again?"

Desperate to make eye contact with Riley—we didn't leave things on the best terms at my house—I twist, needing to see his face as he lingers behind us. But he hurriedly brushes past me, keeping his head down.

"Yup, I'm a prisoner here. I'm not allowed to be on my own." Riley's voice is heavy with anguish as he carefully chooses the chair at the end of the long table, far away from me.

"If I remember correctly, supreme?" Bree asks Riley.

Riley shakes his head as Bree slides an overflowing plate of heavily topped pizza and steaming breadsticks in front of him. His eyes stay fixated on his plate as he focuses all his attention on the food in front of him.

Just look at me, Riley. Just for one second.

Margo's eyes soften, empathy emitting from her as her gaze shifts between my boyfriend and me.

"So, Izzy, how's your dad?" Tahlia asks.

"He's not good. I wanted to stay, but they wouldn't let me since he's in the ICU."

"That's lame," Jessa chimes in.

"Very lame," I agree.

Callen crosses behind me. His energy radiates through me, humming in my cells. He's so close, but then the feeling gradually dissipates the further he walks away from me. I steal a glance as he grabs a slice of peperoni pizza. Our eyes accidently meet, and he flashes me a protective grin. I quickly drop my gaze.

I can't entertain our connection.

Not right now.

Not in front of Riley.

"I heard you like cheese and black olives." Bree slides a plate in front of me, motioning for me to take a seat. Her intricate hunter's tattoo that's weaved around her arm crosses my line of sight.

I take a step back to wait for her to walk away before taking my place at the table.

"Um, yes. That's my go-to." I nervously smile, setting my overnight bag on the ground next to me. I place my backpack with the spellbook over my lap, discreetly under the table.

"Izzy, I hope your dad pulls through this. The girls told me there's a chance he may need a kidney transplant if things continue to go south. Does your dad have any other relatives you can contact if that's the necessary measure? I'd hate to see you have to give up one of your kidneys at your age, although that's not unheard of, and it might be the only option," Bree says.

My hand drops below my ribcage, pressing firmly where I believe my kidneys are. I was never good at biology. The idea of surgery has me feeling queasy. I would much rather hold on to both of my kidneys if possible.

"No, it's just me and him."

The moment I say the words, I'm taken back to Anna in the clearing—*find Jonathan Kent*. The man who I think could be my grandfather. The man who Anna saved by abandoning him before he could fall in love with her. Could it be possible he has two healthy kidneys with one to spare for his long-lost son? But hopefully, it doesn't come down to that. My dad will pull through this—he has to. I can't entertain any other outcome.

When I look up, everyone seems to be staring at me. I didn't realize the attention I'm drawing to myself.

"Izzy, your dad is going to be OK," Margo sweetly says.

"I know he will. He's strong." I grin back at my friend.

"So, hemlock?" Bree says, moving her attention to her husband.

"That's what the doctor said Steven ingested. Something's not sitting right with me about it, though," Barrett responds, his voice tinged with concern.

Bree scrunches her tiny nose upward, like there's an unpleasant scent in the air. "That sounds like a witch's doing."

I unintentionally raise my gaze to meet Callen's intense, dark eyes. His eyes scan my face steadily, searching for any signs of the inner turmoil that Bree's words provoked. I remain expressionless, knowing my efforts are in vain—he knows my thoughts. He can sense I'm rattled.

"Blame it on a witch, Mom. It's always a witch's doing," Callen taunts, speaking up for the witches that are too afraid to confront the beautiful huntress in the room.

"Witches can be callous creatures, as we all know. Look at Elizabeth Crowley," she taunts back.

"Yeah, but that's just one witch. You can't judge them all based on one bad seed," Callen responds.

"Witches have given themselves this bad rap. They're known

to use all the earth's gifts, even the deadly ones. Hemlock is a witch's favorite."

"Isn't that stereotyping?" Callen asks.

"Not when it's a fact," she responds. "History has shown it time and time again. It's an easy thing to serve your enemy."

"But my dad's not the enemy," I protest.

"That's very true. As far as we're all concerned, Steven Beswick hasn't crossed a witch with bad intentions. So, why would a witch want to harm him?" Barrett responds.

"Hello, aren't you all forgetting something? Something huge! Anna's back from the dead. It had to have been her!" I shout.

"Perhaps," Bree responds. "We'll continue to monitor the situation, but I don't think Anna would hurt her own child."

"Monitor the situation! You've got to be kidding me. Wasn't that what you were supposed to be doing when my dad got sick? I don't think you're monitoring the situation very well. Because if you were, then my dad wouldn't have been poisoned, and you'd know where Anna was right now, then we could finally ask her for ourselves."

"The kid has a good point," Barrett says, stroking his chin.

"We've never had to deal with this kind of situation before, Barrett," Bree hisses. "You can't blame us for trying." She turns to me, her voice firm and direct.

"I just don't understand how one person can be dead and then not. Even if that person is a witch. It doesn't make sense," I respond.

"Izzy, none of this makes any sense. But I don't think Anna would hurt Steven," Bree adds.

"Are you not hearing the words I'm saying? It can't be Anna that came back. It's something else."

"You sound crazy, Izzy. People don't come back from the dead." Bree's fingers clench the edge of the countertop, her frustration with me building with each word.

"Let's just hope no one else gets hurt by Anna," I grumble the words with a hint of resentment. I glance to Barrett. I get a sense he doesn't agree with his wife.

"Maybe our eyes were all playing tricks on us. We experienced something horrific, and magic was involved. It's hard to say for certain, but maybe she wasn't dead. When my parents moved her body, they woke her. You weren't close to Anna, so maybe she left without saying goodbye. It's probably not the first time she's done something like that, right? Then maybe your dad simply came into contact with the plant," Tahlia says, trying to make sense of a senseless situation.

These are all thoughts that have lashed through my mind, but now with my dad resting in a hospital bed, I can't help but think we've all been naïve. Our eyes aren't opened to all possibilities. We're supernatural beings— well, most of us. We should be the most open to things outside of normal comprehension. If we can't be open-minded to all possibilities, then we're screwed.

"But this brings us to our other order of business," Barrett says, lingering on his words. "Tim."

"What about him?" I hastily question.

Bree's face is emotionless with her reply. "We're letting him go in the morning."

Fire boils under my skin. "Um, no, you're not. He killed Anna. Are you insane?"

"Well, since things have changed, and Anna isn't dead, he didn't commit a crime," she responds.

"He confessed to killing Isobel, and he wanted to kill us. You said it yourself that he put your children in danger. You have a treaty or whatever."

"Well, that might be true, but there are other factors at play now. With your dad being sick, it would look bad if Tim didn't visit. Also, Megan's funeral is tomorrow. All the officers will be attending. We can't keep up this ruse. We didn't have a good plan; now it's slowly unraveling, due to things outside of our control."

"Did you know about this?" I huff at Riley.

"No, Izzy. I swear I didn't know a thing about this." Riley finally looks at me and firmly responds, "I don't agree with them."

"Are you two crazy?" Callen's voice rises in exasperation as he gestures toward his parents.

Jessa, Tahlia, and Margo are speechless; their eyes wide and mouths agape as they stare at Bree in disbelief.

"What if he tries to kill me again? What if he goes after your son or daughter?" I cry out, my body trembling with apprehension.

"Don't worry, we'll make sure he doesn't," Bree says.

"Tell me how you're going to do that. I don't think a hunter has the kind of control you think they do. Riley nearly attacked me an hour ago!" I shout.

"What? Riley, how could you?" With an open hand, Jessa

reaches across Margo and strikes Riley with a loud slap.

I flinch at the sound of her hand smacking against his cheek, but I can't help but swell with pride at my friend's loyalty. I never expected this from Jessa of all people.

"I didn't mean to," he stammers, his eyes downcast in shame.

"My point exactly," I answer, my sorrowful gaze making a silent plea to my boyfriend for forgiveness in tossing him under the bus like that.

"Riley is a baby hunter, still unaware of how to harness his desires. We'll train him. I'm not saying it will be easy. But Izzy, I'm standing here as a hunter in my kitchen, serving a group of witches pizza that I generously paid for. I'm allowing you all to be in my home, and have I once tried to attack you?"

"Well, no."

"Control comes with time. Tim will be good. I'll make sure of it."

"I wish I could believe you."

"It's what we need to do. But for tonight, the two of you will be separated. Girls, you'll sleep in the large guest room together. And Riley, we'll lock you into the smaller guest room," Bree says.

"Oh, great, an upgraded cage," Riley gripes.

CHAPTER 20
DAGGER TO MY HEART

The guest room is even larger than I expected, with high ceilings and ornate crown molding. I take a step into the room and curl my toes into the plush carpet, feeling its warmth and luxuriousness. I haven't felt this kind of lavishness in a while. It feels good, and I find a bit of comfort in that. I take what I can get these days.

Tahlia retrieves four sleeping bags from an expansive walk-in closet and places them next to the bed.

"Better grab one more," a voice calls out from the doorway.

I whip around, annoyed to see Callen leaning against the wall.

Can't he give me a moment to breathe?

"What are you doing in here?" Tahlia huffs. "No boys allowed."

"I'm not letting you go unprotected all night with Riley down the hall."

"His door's locked like some kind of animal. Don't you think that's enough protection?" I question.

"Can't be too safe these days. Izzy, aren't you forgetting he had you pinned against the wall just hours ago? If I hadn't come to your rescue, who knows what would have happened?"

"I told you I had things under control."

"How do the two of you keep ending up together?" Jessa asks quizzically, while judgmentally staring at me.

"Magic," Callen says with a laugh.

I know he's not ready to tell our secret because that would mean acknowledging the intense connection that witches can create. Even if my connection with Callen is more powerful than what I have with my friends, I can't risk it. Margo and I have sensed its presence, but she's not fully aware of its power. As long as I'm keeping the dark truth from coming out that Jessa was the one who killed the sweet girl they're about to lay to rest, I can't share my knowledge of this bond. The thought of having to keep this secret from her is like a dagger to my heart, yet I know it's for the greater good of our coven.

"Whatever, you're so annoying," Jessa huffs.

"Back at ya, blondie," Callen responds, taking a small step into the room.

Tahlia's eyes flutter as she rolls them, their mossy green color shimmering against the soft lighting. "Can you two quit with it for a moment? Seriously." She plops down onto one of the rolled up sleeping bags, perfectly balancing herself. She lets her head fall into her hands with her wild curls dangling from her ponytail. When she lifts her head, her gaze meets her brother's. "I suppose since you're here we could use your help." A tear falls from one eye, leaving a streak. "I can't become like Tim and Riley, or even Mom. I just can't. We have to find a way to break this stupid hunter's curse, so I can live a normal fucking life."

"Well, somewhat normal. You might be a witch, remember?" My response is buoyed by a small spark of hope.

"I'd rather be a witch. None of you have the urge to kill your friends."

None of the witches in the room respond. Instead, we all produce our best sympathetic expressions, giving Tahlia her moment.

I clear my throat, changing the direction of focus, because after all, I have a piece of hope to offer. "So, I looked through the spellbook, and there isn't anything about breaking the hunter's curse, but I have this." I produce Isobel's diary from my bag, setting it on the plush carpet.

The five of us huddle around the small item, taking a seat in a perfect circle.

"What's that?" Tahlia asks.

"It's Isobel's diary. Riley found it among Tim's things and gave it back to me. Tim tried to steal it a second time the day he came to attack us. But I made sure to take it back. It doesn't belong to him. It's mine, but I can't read it without you all. Well, I mean I tried to read it when it first came to me, but I couldn't see all the passages. I can't help but think Isobel used this to document life after her banishment."

The atmosphere sparks with a charge of excitement; the walls practically vibrate with anticipation. A feeling of déjà vu hits me as my friends stare optimistically at the diary placed in the center of our group. The sight brings me back to the day we found the spellbook. The day our lives changed.

Now, we gaze upon a new item, hoping it satisfies us with never seen before secrets and answers. Our last chance to help Tahlia and Riley and save our friendships from impending doom.

"What do the first entries say?" Jessa asks.

"Well, in her first entries, she talked about life in the colony. It was hard, and she hinted that she knew she was different, but she was too afraid to say anything, even too afraid to write it down." I pick up the book and hand it to Jessa. "Here, read it for yourselves."

They go around in a circle, each taking turns reading the first passages in Isobel's diary.

"Wow, she knew what she was and couldn't tell a soul in fear of persecution," Margo says.

"My heart kind of breaks for her. She doesn't seem evil or ill willed in these passages. She's just afraid. Also, did you see she referenced the lady of potions? That's Elizabeth Crowley," I respond.

"This witchy web keeps weaving tighter. Everything seems to be connected," Margo responds.

When the diary finds its way back to me, I brush my fingertips against the faded words, anticipating a transformation in the ink, but nothing occurs. I'm slightly surprised the ink doesn't obey my touch because we're all together like Isobel asked.

Callen watches me intently as I make another attempt, but again, nothing happens.

"Perhaps we need a magical incantation to make this happen. She wants us to work for it. She cautiously kept her words hidden, concealing her confessions. You'd think that whoever could find the key, so to speak, would be the one to view her entries," Callen replies.

"Always pushing spellwork, aren't you, Callen?" I taunt.

Callen doesn't respond because I know he feels bad for the protection spell not working. And he should.

Margo tilts her head to one side, giving Callen a curious expression. "We need a key?"

Callen shakes his head. "Margo, I don't mean a literal key—a spell being the key in this scenario."

"Oh," she meekly replies.

In true Margo fashion, her mood shifts and a glow of excitement spreads across her face. She leaps to her feet, strides across the room, then bends down in the far corner. The sound of plastic bags being shuffled around bleeds into the air. She proudly swaggers back to us with her arms bursting from our purchases from Invoke Awakenings. The sight of their logo on the bags makes my stomach curl— *"You have a dark spirit around you, girl. There is something attached to your dark shadow."*

I shake the black-haired woman's words from my mind, but they're still there, waiting to taunt me again when I'm vulnerable.

Callen's hand moves toward my backpack as he softly asks, "May I?"

I nod, and he slides the spellbook out.

Margo's shriek invades the air. "You've been lugging that thing around with you all day?"

"Yes, and my back hurts."

"Maybe there's a spell for backaches," Margo jokes.

"Probably," I respond.

Margo holds out a plethora of candles. "Which color?"

The pink candle is among the ones to choose from. I want Margo to ask him what it's used for, but she doesn't.

"Blue. It's to promote open communication," he responds.

"I need something to set these on, so they don't tip over and burn down your house," Margo asks, looking to Tahlia.

"Oh, and T find some ribbon to make a circle. Mom would kill us if we got salt in her carpet," Callen adds. "And grab a tiny bowl of water, along with the house plant at the end of the hallway."

"Geez, anything else, your highness?" Tahlia asks, closing the door before Callen can add to her ever-growing list. After a couple of trips back to the room, she's gathered all the requested supplies.

"Lock the door." Callen nods to his sister. "Mom and Dad will freak if they knew what we're doing in here."

Tahlia rolls her eyes, but she does as her brother requests.

Callen flips the book open, his eyes scanning over every page as he searches for the perfect spell. "I think I found one that will work. A decloaking spell might do the trick."

"Um. Hello! What am I supposed to do while you guys play witch?" Jessa asks, letting out a piteous whimper.

"You're just as important as any of us. You need to observe and make sure everyone remains safe. But maybe you should watch from the bed. We can't have you getting too close and getting sick again," I respond.

Jessa climbs onto the bed, taking her place, perched on

the edge, ready to be our watchful guardian.

Margo carefully lights four of the blue candles. The flames grow high, dancing across the four walls of the guest room. She lays the ribbon in a circle the best she can. She places a few more items in the middle, including the plant, bowl of water, and some other things we bought at the store.

I quickly do a mental checklist, making sure all the elements are accounted for.

Fire—the candles.

Water—the tiny bowl of tap water from the kitchen.

Earth—the plant.

Air—pretty sure we're breathing it.

OK. I feel better knowing we're more prepared for this spell than the one last night.

Margo, Callen, Tahlia, and I step inside the circle. We greet each other with warm smiles. Margo lights a bundle of white sage and walks it around our circle, letting the ash fall into the seashell. We each take turns cleansing ourselves with the smoke.

"Do we need to do the blood thing?" Margo asks, looking to Callen for the answer.

"It can only help, right?" he responds, picking up the athame. "All we need is a tiny bit of blood as an offering. Please don't hurt yourselves too much."

He makes a tiny incision in his hand, letting the blood drip into the small black bowl we bought at the store. Each of us takes our turn, ending with me. With a flick of the blade, I blend our blood and place the bowl next to our open spellbook. I lay Isobel's diary open, exposing the faded pages.

As we link hands, I hear a faint crackle in the air, then the familiar energy surges between the four of us. We recite the spell in unison, fervently chanting it three times. The words seem to bounce off the walls in a wave of sound.

"Hail to the guardian of mother earth, hear us.
Hail to the guardian of powerful air, hear us.
Hail to the guardian of rageful fire, hear us.
Hail to the guardian of intuitive water, hear us now.
We beseech you to show us what's hidden in plain sight.
We call upon you to shed some light.
Hide you must not.
Guardians, be blessed, and be with us through our reveal.

So shall it be."

Our four hands remain intertwined. All I can hear is the sound of our breathing as we silently stare at the diary—waiting for something to happen.

The bed next to us groans as Jessa shifts her weight, but I don't pay attention to her. My eyes remain glued to the unchanged ink.

Come on. Please work.

The faded words begin to darken and come to life on the page. An excited shriek escapes my lips. "It's working. Are you guys seeing this?"

The four of us drop to our knees.

"It freakin' worked. We're magical together," Tahlia yelps with delight.

"Fingers crossed we find some answers," I say, peering down at the book.

We huddle together, each of us eagerly scanning the page with our eyes, hoping for answers in the darkened words.

CHAPTER 21
A WITCH'S CONFESSION

JULY 1691

The Lady of Potions came into the village today. There was talk amongst the townsfolk that her potions are poisonous. But I think she wants to help people. I get a strange feeling when she is around me. It is hard to describe, so maybe I should not.

Days are short, and the nights are long. My harvest is unrewarding, and death is everywhere, including my crops. The reverend claims he is leading us down the path of virtuous intentions, ridding us of our sins, but I feel his intentions are not that of virtue. I cannot speak my thoughts though because that would be a sin. It is the devil's talk, but is not the devil already here? We are all suffering, so what is the point in doing things with virtuous intentions?

AUGUST 1691

The reverend says a lady of my age should be married and I will feel pure once I take my vows. I am to be wed the Sunday after next to William Williams. It is horrid for a man's surname to be the same as his first. That should be a sin. He is an awful man with a vile temper. I spit on his name and his temper. I do not want to marry him, but

I will perish if I do not, as winter is coming, and he has a plentiful farm. I will marry William Williams out of survival, not out of love.

The Lady of Potions called to me last night. She spoke to me in a dream. She possesses the knowledge I seek, yet I cannot go to her, for I fear she is what the old world called a witch. How else would she be in my dreams? I will not allow her to penetrate the depths of my soul. But she said she could free me from the life I have been fated to live.

SEPTEMBER 1691

I am now a married woman, but I despise the man I am vowed to. William Williams is selfish and cold-hearted; he treats me with disrespect and contempt. He wants a son. I am not sure how much longer I can fend off this abhorrent man.

Today we gathered in the village as the reverend deemed some of the town's women unfit. The colony is pulling apart, and fear is spreading like a disease. No woman may speak backhanded to a man, although I wish I could. I must bite my tongue, or I too will be called out as unfit.

"If thou disrespect, thou are shunned," the reverend preached.

I watched as the men loaded the women into wagons and paraded them through town as punishment. Public humility for those who question the path.

OCTOBER 1691

William Williams told the reverend of my backhanded talk. They came for me today, but I ran into the dark forbidden forest. The Lady of Potions was waiting for me. She knew I would come eventually. Her name is Elizabeth Crowley. Her husband is dead as of four years.

She has been outcasted by society, but I think she prefers it that way. She told me I am special, and there are others like me. She talked of potions and chants to heal our colony's women of their ill-fitted fates.

She said no one is going to save us but ourselves.

Her words are blasphemous, and my ears should burn, yet I believe her. So, if that makes me a sinner, then I am a sinner.

She offered me a purple potion to ease my stress. I drank it. All of it. She said a funny prayer for me, then sent me on my way.

NOVEMBER 1691

Elizabeth wrote me a note asking to meet in the forest. When I arrived, two other women were there. Lydia Bishop and Dinah Abbott. She tested each of us separately. We all passed the tests. Although, I get the feeling I was more powerful than the others. Together, we are strong and we can do things. Things I cannot even write about because they seem untrue.

I have been practicing when William Williams is out.

DECEMBER 1691

I am a witch. I cannot deny it. I am powerful and I can do things with my thoughts. The power has always been there. I was born with it; I realize that now. Elizabeth seems jealous of my gifts, but she needs me. There must be four, she says.

JANUARY 1692

I keep William Williams away with chants I recite while he sleeps. I am well fed and safe from him, but the outside world is still a frightening place, and I must hide my true self.

Two children in the village are having the fits. I feel in my bones that something terrible is coming. There is a shift in the wind.

FEBRUARY 1692

Another child is having the fits. At service, the mother said the girl's body contorted into a strange position, and she made peculiar sounds. They say the girls are afflicted. The devil has them. They called out three women as being witches, but I know witches, and these women aren't. I fear each time I enter our sacred place, I will burn in front of the entire congregation, but it never happens. So, is what I'm doing all that wrong?

The Wives of Salem Coven is what we call ourselves now. We meet often and record our chants. We could help the children, but the fear is growing like a disease, and witches are to blame, yet it was not a witch that afflicted these children.

MARCH 1692

Witches are here to do the devil's work, the afflicted say. More women are named by the children. They have it all wrong.

My powers are strong, stronger than my coven mates, making me their High Priestess. I was chosen, but I fear this is not what the others were expecting.

APRIL 1692

William Williams walked right off the roof. Just like I wished he'd do, but I cast no such desire with herbs or chants. I fear Elizabeth Crowley took my words and used them to harm me. Her dark side is ever present and growing darker with resentment, as I am more powerful than she. She is no longer drawing from the earth's gifts, but rather from malevolent forces to cause harm to those who have harmed us. Does she know the damage she has done, for soon they will come for me? She talks of séances and communicating with the dead to learn from their mistakes, but I fear she has lost her mind. Maybe she is afflicted like the children.

MAY 1692

They came for me today as I knew they would. They said I killed my husband by way of witchcraft. People said they saw him walk off the roof as if someone was telling him to do it. I denied the claims, but it is useless. Soon, they will test me as a witch, and I will fail. I am more powerful than they could ever realize.

Although their tests are ill-fitted for my gifts and foolish, they will still see what I am because that is what they want to see.

I am grateful I have my diary in this cell. I shoved it into my pantaloons when I saw them coming for me. They might find it, and I will be hanged for it, but it is better than being truly alone, for the outcome will be the same. I may not have killed my husband, but I am a witch, and that crime is paid for with death.

JUNE 1692

Each day, the cell grows tighter as more witches are rounded up and brought here to await their tests. The cell is dirty and smells of urine. The rats are becoming larger and seem better fed than us. The tiny scraps of bread hardly fill my stomach, and I ache all over. Dinah Abbott and Lydia Bishop arrived a couple of weeks ago. We've been planning our escape, but not the kind that involves walking out the door.

Elizabeth Crowley arrived yesterday. I am unsure of her crimes as she has not spoken much since her arrival, but we are stronger together, so it should work.

JULY 1692

Elizabeth is away being tested. It has been longer than most. The guards have been more cruel than usual. Dinah is nearing death and has not eaten in days, but they do not care if we suffer. We must act with haste, or our chance to leave will be gone.

JULY 1692

We are cloaked, always nearby, but doomed in our purgatory because of one woman's ill will toward her own kind. We have been cursed three times over. I am afraid that is all I will write for a while.

AUGUST 1788

We are free to leave, but I am not ready to emerge. I have been perfecting my craft, and my bloodline will be stronger if I stay. I am not ready for this pretentious world. Dinah and Lydia left me, but that is fine. We have grown apart during our many years together. We do not see things eye to eye anymore. I fear my resentment toward Elizabeth has toiled my connections with the others.

It is lonely as I watch the world go by.

JANUARY 1941

My dearest diary, I have longed for the sound of my quill scratching against paper, but I saw no need to write. Life has been mired in stillness as I waited for the perfect moment to return. I am the most powerful witch, my bloodline the purest of all. I have earned my power, and no one can challenge me. Well, except for the lingering curses, but at least I survived my first sentencing.

But now it is time to deal with the second part of Elizabeth Crowley's condemnation, for my bloodline has been forsaken.

I have found comfort and security in the embrace of a kind man. After all, I need a provider. Markus Thompson owns a stunning house perched atop a hill, giving a majestic view of the town. I am thankful for his companionship. Turns out I am a looker, and the 1940s fit me well. His compliments are engorging my ego as I have heard the townsfolk say, but who knows how much time we will be gifted for his love for me grows each day, putting his life in peril.

I find it refreshing that women can own property now. This will work to my advantage if things do not turn out well for my soon-to-be husband. It is too bad he is my first test because I have grown rather fond of him. He is nothing like William Williams.

The legacies of The Wives of Salem Coven and Elizabeth Crowley's monsters have yet to catch wind of my return. I fear the magic is gone in my coven mates' bloodlines, for no one has passed it down properly. I hoped to seek them out to assist with my tests, but they seem to be worthless. The Latham and Hawkins' bloodlines found their way to East Gate some time ago. Although, I am not sure they understand why they chose to settle here as no witches seemed to be ripe for the hunt. A nice little loophole I have found over the years. A hunter may sense a witch, but until they show signs of magic, they are safe from the kill.

Once I let my magic unleash, I am fair game, and it will be hunting season. I am the prey. They will find me, and they will come. But now is not the time to worry myself.

I must remain focused and test the curse that fates the existence of my bloodline. I have watched Lydia and Dinah's families through the turmoil of loss after loss, century after century. I will find a way to break this curse, even if I am alone in doing so.

However, I shall remain guiltless and unstained. This is not my fault, and no blood shall be on my hands.

Isobel Opal Beswick of East Gate Connecticut

The Bloodline Curse Tests

Markus Thompson 1942

Henry Hancock 1946

Robert Tucker 1958

APRIL 1958
Anna arrived- second generation.
Robert Tucker would have made a fine father. I was sad to see him part with this world. This curse is turning out to be unbreakable. But at least I am not alone anymore. I have my baby girl.

The Bloodline Curse Tests- Part two

Frank Hermiston 1960

Hank Becker 1962

Timothy Palmer 1976

DECEMBER 1976
I have failed. My daughter does not understand my need to pursue this quest. I am doing all of this for us. She is pulling away from me.

I feel it. I need her magic, but she refuses. She is as worthless to me as the others.

JANUARY 1977

Steven arrived- third generation.

My daughter does not understand her legacy and what being a Beswick means. She left East Gate and her boyfriend behind, thinking it will save him. Only time will tell. I miss my sweet grandson, but I know he will come back to me.

JULY 1984

My daughter pretends as if we aren't witches, and it breaks my heart. Everything I've done for this family, and there is no respect. This past quick visit, my sweet grandson Steven showed no signs of magic, and not for a lack of trying on my part. I attempted to coax the magic out of him. I've made a safe space for him to practice out in the woods. We made a fort where his mother couldn't find us, but still nothing came. Perhaps he's too young and distracted. However, it's probably for his own good. He's befriended the young Hawkins boy, Timothy.

JANUARY 2003

With the invention of that blasphemous thing they call the internet, my years have been toiled with growing hate. People can search just about anything, including marriage certificates. I've shown no signs of witchcraft in public, but locals find it fun to poke at my painful history of dead lovers, making me the town witch. Why else could I possibly have so many dead husbands? It must be witchcraft, they say. They're right, but all this has done is cause the hunters to look my way. They're just waiting for the right time.

I don't go out much these days. But I do enjoy when Steven visits. Thankfully, he hasn't questioned any of the rumors. He has a wife now. She's pretty and kind, but I don't get too attached.

DECEMBER 2004

Izzy arrived — fourth generation.

I felt her arrival before she was born. She is the connection I've been missing this whole time. My dearest namesake will be the one to take over our legacy. There is hope. I feel it in my bones. She will be the chosen one. Soon, when she's ready, the Beswicks will regain their place. She will be the one to break the curse.

Steven's been blessed with more love than a Beswick is entitled. I'm happy for him, but every day I fear the worst.

My dearest diary, I've been keeping a close eye on the others. I'm excited to report I have a new sense of hope, but there is an abomination that's come to my attention. Dinah's bloodline has married and mated with a Latham bloodline hunter. I feel ill as I write the words. I must keep an eye on the Latham-Hart family as they've spawned two half-breeds. Such a hybrid has never existed. I'm curious and will keep a watchful eye.

JULY 2010

Izzy is special. She can be called when the time is right.

I saw the half-breeds today at the market. The hunter's eyes wandered, but she kept to herself. I tested the children when she walked away, and the boy answered. I don't have high hopes for the girl, although very pretty, she will make an ugly hunter.

SEPTEMBER 2016

The curse has taken another. My poor Steven is broken. I wish I could tell him I tried. But it's safer if he doesn't know.

As for Lydia's bloodline, the Hawley girl is promising. Still no hope for the half-breed girl, which is disappointing.

MAY 2017

I fear my time in this realm is nearing its end. I need the girl to come. She is the key to unlocking everything. There is more at play here than meets the eye.

CHAPTER 22
A WAR IS COMING

The growing knot in my stomach tightens. I turn the page, disturbed and conflicted by Isobel's story. Early on, I felt a twinge of pity for her, but that emotion was extinguished by her confession of willingly killing all her husbands to test spells she knew could only work with four bloodline witches.

"This can't be it," I say, jerking the pages over one by one, the sound of disappointment ringing in my ears as every page I flip comes up blank. "There needs to be more. There just has to be. She never mentioned trying to break the hunter's curse."

My heart sinks as I let my head fall forward, afraid to face my friends after failing them. This was my Hail Mary—my last idea—and it provided us with no answers. All that's confirmed is that Isobel knew what we all were. She was aware of everything. She put me in harm's way to get what she wanted, and I'm no closer to the answers I seek.

I can hardly bear the sound of the soft cries slipping from Tahlia, another reminder that time isn't on our side. I'm failing. I wanted—I needed—to save Riley and Tahlia. I really thought Isobel had the answer.

"You saw what she wrote about me. I wasn't called like Callen," Tahlia says between sobs.

"But Tahlia, our spells worked with you. You're our fourth. Isobel didn't live long enough to realize your potential. You were a late bloomer," Margo responds.

"I want to believe you," Tahlia says.

"To be honest, I expected more," I admit, letting my gaze meet my friends. "I'm actually pretty pissed right now. That's right, Isobel, my dearest Gran-gran, if you're here right now, how could you do this to me? You pushed us all together, so we could break the bloodline curse. You must have figured out a way for us to break the hunter's curse, so we could live in peace. Otherwise, what's the point if none of us can live happy lives? There has to be a way to break the hunter's curse."

The smell of ink fills the air. Words appear on the open blank page below as if someone is writing in real time.

There is only one way to break the hunter's curse.
And that is by death.

All the hunters must die, or all bloodline witches must die.

Uncontrolled emotion engulfs me, leaving me seething with sadness and rage. I glance back to the page below, hoping my mind is playing tricks on me again. But the words are there, clear as day.

It's us or them.

I look to Tahlia, and her eyes brim with tears. "No, that can't be the final answer."

My heart sinks to the pit of my stomach. I really hoped Isobel had the answers, but it turns out the only way to break the curse is if we all die, or all the hunters die. I know our death is more likely than theirs. I'm afraid to say the words out loud because it makes it more final.

"The hunters have been breeding for years, and there's no way to wipe out their bloodline, not that we would do that. As for us, the bloodline witches, it's only me, my dad, Callen, maybe Tahlia, Margo, Margo's mom, and Anna, if she's really alive. Those numbers don't look good for us witches."

"Look, more is appearing," Margo softly says, drawing our attention back to the book.

A war is coming.

Someone you all know has betrayed you.

You must save Anna to save Steven.

My hand shakily points to the page. "Callen, it's just like my tarot card—the future. The seven of wands showed a person ready for battle. What kind of war is coming?"

Callen's jaw is noticeably tight; he's just as shaken as I am. He forcibly swallows before answering me. "I don't want to admit that crazy woman could be right about any of this, but she might be on to something. Remember, she asked you if you were preparing for a competition in your future? What if she meant war?"

"But who betrayed us? Tim? We already know that," I say.

"And how can we save Anna if we don't know where she is?" Margo asks.

"What do you want from us?" I shout into thin air. "Could you please be a little more specific?"

Slowly, an image springs to life on the page, gradually revealing itself as the ink continues to spread.

"What is it?" Tahlia asks.

"That's my necklace," Margo says, clutching her pendant tightly. "What does my pendant have to do with anything?"

"You did say it was a family heirloom. Could it have belonged to Lydia Bishop?" Tahlia asks.

"I suppose it could have," Margo responds.

I shiver as a gust of cold air whips around me, flipping the book shut.

Margo lets out a shrill, ear-piercing scream. "Izzy, there's something behind you. Don't move."

Her words immobilize me, rooting me into place. I take a shuddering breath, my heart pounding in my chest. I slowly turn to look over my shoulder, when I hear the low, ragged breathing of something in the shadows behind me.

Darkness descends upon the room as the overhead light snaps and fizzles out. The flames of the candles flicker, dying, leaving the room in total blackness. Unease fills my body, leaving my skin crawling with goosebumps. My heart stops, and I feel an icy breath on my neck.

"Help me, Izzy."

"Anna," I gasp out her name, my breath catching in my throat.

"I'm trapped. Save my soul."

With a sudden flicker, the lights turn on, and Margo shrieks again.

I whip my head around, and a chill flushes down my spine. I catch a ghostly sight of Anna, dressed in a long, ethereal, white gown, hovering behind me. A heavy, smoldering scent of ash permeates the air. Wild, orangish-red flames lick her feet before dancing their way up her body until she's completely consumed, vanishing without a trace.

"What the hell was that?" I scream.

CHAPTER 23
A DARK SPIRIT

The four of us abandon our circle in horror, frantically launching ourselves on to the bed next to Jessa with our fear hovering in the air like a heavy fog.

"What the hell did I just witness?" Jessa shrieks. "I was calling to you guys, but you couldn't hear me. I was trying to stop it—to end whatever that was, but I couldn't."

"What was that thing?" Tahlia asks, her voice laced with panic.

"Th-that was Anna, right?" I stutter.

"No, before Anna showed up and burned in front of us. Izzy, you didn't see what we all saw because your back was turned," Margo says, her voice quivering. "There was something black—like a shadow behind you, hissing in your ear."

A chill creeps up my spine, sending a wave of terror through my body. "A dark spirit," I respond, still haunted by the tarot lady's words. The look in her eyes made it clear that she saw it too. I suppose I don't blame her for asking me to leave now.

"What does it want?" Margo asks.

"I think it has something to do with Anna. I think whatever that dark spirit is, it has her soul trapped somewhere."

"Well then, how the hell is she walking around?" Callen asks with confusion etched across his face.

"I don't know, but that thing—Anna incarnated—it tried to kill my dad. We have to stop it before it does more damage. And the only way to do that is to communicate with her soul. It's the only way to find out how to stop this. The real Anna is hurting; you all saw it."

"And how the hell are we going to do that?" Tahlia asks.

"Please tell me we're going to do a séance or something cool," Jessa squeals with inappropriate delight.

I roll my eyes at Jessa's inconsideration. But she's right. I think it's our only option.

"Um, no, not a great idea. We can't play with that kind of magic," Margo interjects. "Plus, I think you're all forgetting we don't know the first thing about communicating with the dead."

"We're witches, and I'm pretty sure we've already been communicating with the dead. This time, it will be on our terms. You saw Isobel's words; we have to save Anna to help my dad."

With a snap, Tahlia flings her hands in the air, her cheeks flushing red. "And what about the hunters? What about me and Riley? Are we just shit out of luck? Riley only has days left."

"Maybe the real Anna can help us figure it out. We need to try and communicate with her. It's our last chance. I have to have some hope," I respond. "I don't know what else we can do. We have to try, at least."

"I don't think this is a good idea. Isn't this dark magic? Isn't this the exact thing Anna warned us of? You read the same diary I did. Even Isobel wasn't pleased that Elizabeth wanted to do such a thing. I highly doubt this is what Anna would want from you," Margo says.

"Well, it might be the thing that saves her soul," I respond.

CHAPTER 24
PANCAKES AND PRISONERS

The morning air hangs thick and still, carrying a feeling of dread as we all make our way into the kitchen. Tim's impending release has my nerves rattled, not to mention my dad's lying in a hospital bed. I wish I was there right now, but visiting hours don't start until eight. So, I have to wait. I feel sick to my stomach, not knowing if my dad will be OK. I wish there was something I could do right now.

Well, there is, but it involves dark magic.

Save Anna to save my dad.

I wish I had a more logical and informed answer to how that is supposed to work. What if we save Anna's soul and it doesn't help my dad? Then what?

Jessa stayed up last night researching séances, but I think some of it is intuitive because there isn't a handbook on this kind of thing. Well, at least not one you can find easily on the internet. Maybe Invoke Awakenings sells a guidebook, but I'm not stepping foot in that store again any time soon.

Riley's already seated at the kitchen table, sitting in the same seat as last night with a grim look upon his face. I flash him a tender smile as I pull out the chair next to his, but the kindness isn't reciprocated. Is he mad at me, or is his instinctive hunter nature becoming more dominant? I want to tell him everything he missed last night, but now isn't the right time.

Callen's protectively watching me from across the kitchen, his stance rigid and alert like a guard on duty. I'm annoyed, but I suppose it's good that someone's looking out for me.

The rest of my friends join us at the table with very few words. Today will be hard for each of them. We're all dealing with life-changing events in some way or another.

Margo, Jessa, Tahlia, and Riley plan to attend Megan's funeral after school. I want to be there, but I'm not emotionally ready to attend, especially without my dad by my side. And there's the added fact that Tim will be there. I can't be in the same room as that man.

Margo's face is long with sorrow, and her eyes are glossy from crying. We all heard her in the shower this morning; her loud sobs carried down the hall and into the guest room. I wish there was something I could do to make it better, but I think she needs to grieve in her own way, and if that means crying in the shower, then she should let it out. I did my fair share of shower crying when my mom died. There's something about the comfort of the warm water streaming down your back while you heave uncontrollably in a safe space. Although, it's always better when you're not in a house filled with people.

Bree is stationed at her eight-burner stove, managing a full breakfast—one to serve all her houseguests, even the one in the cage. The clang of metal pots and pans is slowly getting under my skin. What I wouldn't do for a little peace and quiet. My world has been nothing but noise and busyness since the start of school.

The smoky smell of bacon drifts through the air, tickling my nose and rousing my appetite.

"It's buffet style this morning, kids," Bree says. "Take a plate and scoop what you want. There's scrambled eggs, toast, bacon, mixed fruit, potatoes, and pancakes."

"Did you even sleep last night, Bree? This must have taken hours. Thank you." Margo reaches for a plate and kicks the buffet line into action.

"It's the least I can do on a day like today." Bree strokes Margo's hair comfortingly as Margo loads up her plate.

Margo is a witch. Bree is a hunter. And she's not trying to kill her over a plate of eggs. Maybe there is some truth in what she said. Hunters can learn control.

I glance to Barrett, who's reading the paper in a nook at the far end of their massive kitchen. He's quiet this morning.

"Do you think one of you could call the school for me and tell them I'm going to be late? I want to go see my dad," I say, directing my question to the adults in the room.

Barrett peeks his head around his paper. "Of course, consider it done. I'll let the school know what's going on with your father and to expect you later today, if at all."

"Thank you, I appreciate that," I respond with a grateful smile, but Barrett's already behind his paper.

Who reads physical newspapers these days? I'm surprised the East Gate paper is still in print. Most things have gone digital, but then again, this town is like taking a step back in time.

I wait until everyone's taken a turn through the buffet line before I get up to make my plate. I can't remember the last time I had homemade pancakes. My mom used to make them all the time with blueberries; it was our Sunday treat. I smile sweetly at the thought. I pile three of them on my plate in her honor, although these pancakes are missing the blueberries. I add a couple pieces of the thick cut bacon because the smell won't let me pass them by.

"Hey, Boss," a deep, throaty voice calls out, making my body tense and freeze in place.

I spin my head around to see the intimidating figure of Sid, the bouncer-like guy. Has he been lurking there the whole time?

"Our prisoner is ready for release," he says.

"OK, good. Let's wait until the kids leave for school."

Suddenly, I don't feel so hungry.

"Will someone take me to the hospital? I'm ready to go now." I let the plate slip from my hands and clatter onto the counter.

Thank goodness it doesn't break. I walk over to Margo and wrap my arm around her from behind, squeezing her tight. "I'll be thinking about you all day."

"Back at you." Margo brings her hand up to mine, and all her sadness flushes through me.

I pull away, grab my backpack, and head for the door, unsure who's taking me to the hospital. I need to get out of this house, so I'm fine walking.

"Hey, Beswick, wait up. I'll drive you."

Callen to the rescue again.

"I'll take her. She's my girlfriend. You've done enough."

Finally, he speaks.

Riley's words hum in my ears as I reluctantly turn around and reenter the kitchen, with all eyes pinning on me.

"I get that, dude, but I don't think that's a good idea," Callen responds, taking a predatory stance between us.

"I don't think you do get that, *dude*. You're always trying to be the hero. I think you've got a thing for my girlfriend." Riley takes an eager step toward Callen, his eyes almost crackling with anger.

I don't know whether to be flattered or scared.

"And what if I do?" Callen responds.

"Come on, guys, not at the kitchen table," Barrett lectures, barely lifting his eyes from his newspaper.

The sound of Jessa snickering hits my eardrums.

I can't let this go any further.

"Hey, guys, can we not do this right now?" I ask, pulling them away from our audience. I shuffle both guys into the living room before the rest of the crew decides to chime in with their opinions.

I firmly stand between the adversaries, my arms sternly crossed under my chest. "Riley is right, Callen. You've been overstepping your bounds."

"You're the one who called me for help the other night, Izzy," Callen says under his breath.

"You called him?" Riley demands, seething with rage. His eyes widen with a frightening intensity.

"I—I didn't want to bother you, Riley. You had enough on your plate."

"Are you choosing him over me?" Riley shakes his head in disbelief.

I uncross my arms and extend my hand toward Riley, but I pause, feeling the palpable anger radiating off him. His emotions are unhinged. I'm well aware of the danger that lurks when his wires get crossed.

"No, it's not like that. I just don't know how safe it is for us to be alone together."

"Well, it sounds like I have my answer. Let the half-breed drive you. You're safer with him. I see where I stand." He pivots to walk away.

"Riley, please don't." I try to grab his arm, but he pulls away, his gaze turning cold as ice.

"Come on, don't let it get to you. He'll understand some day."

"Whatever. I'm still mad at you." I walk outside, letting the door slam behind me.

CHAPTER 25
BLOOD RED

Callen gives me a few moments before meeting me outside. I think he's learning to give me at least a few seconds of space when I'm huffy. Especially when it involves Riley.

He remotely unlocks the door and starts the engine. When I open the car door, the unmistakable scent of hot, stale air fills my nostrils. The scorching heat seems to hang in the air without respite.

"When will this heat wave be over?"

"It's not usually this hot so late in the season. It will end soon."

"I hope so," I respond, fanning myself with my hand. I take it upon myself to adjust the air in the car, turning it to maximum coolness.

"Are you going to drive or just sit here in the driveway all day?" I ask.

"First, I need you to know how truly sorry I am for everything, and not just about my fight with Riley. Even though I remain firm on my stance of keeping you away from him for the time being. But, Izzy, I want to tell you how sorry I am about your dad. I thought he'd be OK. I don't know what we did wrong. I've never had a spell backfire like that. We're bloodline witches; our magic should be stronger together."

"Well, it *did* backfire, and badly. My dad was left unprotected, and our second layer of protection—your parents—didn't help."

"My dad saved your dad's life!"

"Just in the nick of time. If he'd been there sooner, he could have seen it happen and stopped it."

"Perhaps." Callen stews in silence for a moment, letting the hum of the engine fill the air between us. "Hey, did you drink any of that tea last night?"

"No, it was gross. I spit it back into my cup. Why?"

"Don't you think that was the perfect opportunity to poison you both? Perhaps that's the reason our spell didn't work because the hemlock was already in his system."

"Holy shit." I slug Callen in the arm.

Oops, bad habit.

"You could be right. I'm sorry. I'm such an ass. I bet the plan was to take both of us out by slipping hemlock into the tea."

He tenderly rubs his shoulder. "Beswick, there's no hard feelings on my end. All I want is to keep you safe, but we have to work on the slugging thing." He grins. "We can only try to move forward and figure out how to keep your dad alive. If you need anything, Izzy, I'm your guy. Please, please know you can always trust me to do the right thing to the best of my ability." He reaches over and squeezes my hand.

"Actually, can you do me a favor? I haven't had time, but I need to try to find someone."

"Sure, who?"

"His name is Jonathan Kent."

"Who's that?"

"Please start driving. I want to get there right at eight." I check the time on the dashboard.

He shifts the car into reverse and backs down the driveway. "OK, so are you going to tell me who this person is?"

"I think he's my dad's father."

His eyebrows draw close together as he squints in confusion. "Huh? I thought it was just you and your dad. I didn't know you had any other family."

"I've never met him, and I pray he's still alive. I think Anna spared him by leaving him before the baby was born. Didn't you notice in Isobel's diary, she said Anna left her boyfriend behind to try and spare his life? She knew she was cursed, so she left him before he could truly love her back. Remember when I told you I saw her in the other realm the day she supposedly died? Well, she told me to find him. I was eventually going to look him up, so I could reconnect him with my dad, but now it might be to save his life."

"Beswick, that's great news. I'll do an extensive online search while I'm waiting for you."

"Callen, you don't have to stay and wait for me. I don't know how long I'm going to be."

"I have the day off, and there isn't any place I'd rather be than waiting here for you."

A gentle feeling of kindness fills me from the inside out.

"Callen, maybe you are good people." I nudge his arm.

"You're good people too, Beswick." He grins.

"Can I ask you a personal question?"

"Sure, anything," Callen responds.

"Why aren't you away at college?"

"I deferred a year. I didn't want to leave knowing my sister would be going through something. I couldn't let her face changing on her own. I'll go next year. My parents weren't happy, but I'm an adult and can make my own choices."

"That's very sweet of you, Callen. Can I ask you something else?"

"Shoot," he responds.

"So, who is that Sid guy exactly?"

He scrunches up his nose, taking a second to answer me. "He's… um… He's our Familiar?"

"Your what?"

"Our Familiar. See, witches through the centuries have been known to have companions. Not all witches, but some. Familiars can be animals, people, or even plants. Most choose animals because it's the easiest choice. Animals are naturally protective creatures and attach themselves to their owners, but humans… that's another thing." He pauses. "Gosh, how do I explain this?" He reaches up and rubs his freshly shaven chin. "So, some humans want to be useful and wish they had special powers, so the closest they'll get is attaching themselves to a witch. In doing so, they feel special, and it helps a witch out. Sid's been willingly compelled to work for our family. His loyalty and trust is with us."

"Isn't that wrong?"

"No, he's chosen this path for himself."

"But you took away his free will."

"Once again, he volunteered his services. Some people want to be special, and this makes them special by proxy. He still has his own life, but his dedication is to us. He must come when needed. He even has a room in our house."

"So, who did you guys think this dude was your whole lives?"

"Uncle Sid."

"He looks nothing like you. He's giant."

"I never really thought much of it."

"My mind is blown right now. Maybe Jessa can be our Familiar. She always wants to be special." I laugh.

"I don't think Jessa could ever give up her free will to serve someone else. It's not in her nature."

"You're telling me."

The rhythmic shaking of my phone against my leg causes me to glance down. "Speaking of Jessa."

I open the message on my screen.

"Look at this." I flash Callen my phone, but he doesn't take his eyes off the road.

"Jessa sent me a text of a red Jeep with a large black bow tied around it. Her parents dropped this off at your house just now. She's spoiled, and hell, so are all of you."

"No, not fair. I'm paying for this with my own money. Well, paying for half the lease with my own money," he says shyly.

"Her insurance money must have come through."

"I doubt it. That's too fast. Her parents probably paid cash outright to buy her a new one to keep her from whining about it."

"They have that kind of money just lying around?"

"Yup. Jessa's family is hella rich. Her dad owns a bunch of businesses around town. There are even rumors that her dad is thinking of tossing his hat in the running as our next mayor."

"Seriously?"

"I'm surprised she didn't tell you that. She tells everyone."

"Great, the soon-to-be mayor's daughter is friends with a coven of witches, and she killed someone. We can't let her get in trouble for Megan's death. At least her new car's red, less chance of seeing blood with her next hit-and-run."

"Izzy!"

I quickly cover my face with my hands. "Oh my gosh, I can't believe I said that. What's wrong with me?"

"Well, it's kind of true. She hit a girl with her car and left the scene. She's not innocent. We just made it look that way," he responds.

Callen slowly eases into a parking spot close to the entrance of the hospital. "Hey, isn't that lady a teacher at East Gate High?"

I look up to see a woman walking in with a full bouquet in her hand.

"What's Mrs. Jamison doing here?"

CHAPTER 26
TANSIES

The woman with bouncy chestnut-brown hair is unmistakably my teacher. She confidently strides into the building, clutching a vase of flowers.

"That's Mrs. Jamison, the history teacher. I have her first period, which she's also missing." I curiously peer out the window.

"Wonder who she's visiting?" Callen asks.

"You know, she gave me so much crap yesterday for being tardy by twenty seconds, and, well, for missing class the other day when you dropped us off late. She even had the audacity to pull me out of class to tell me she was worried about me. Then she proceeded to tell me she was friends with Isobel and asked about Anna." I squirm in my seat, recalling the encounter with my teacher.

"That's very strange. I didn't think Isobel had any friends."

"Exactly, that's what I said to her. Apparently, Isobel helped her grieve her dead husband."

"That doesn't sound like the Isobel I've heard stories about."

"I know."

"Maybe we'll run into her, and we can ask her more about her friendship with your Gran-gran."

"Let's do it," I respond, with my hand already on the door handle.

Inside the hospital, my eyes whiz around, searching for signs of Mrs. Jamison amid the bustling activity. I wonder if hospitals ever have a quiet moment, or are they always this busy?

"We must have just missed her. I don't see her anywhere." I toss my hands in defeat.

Callen points to the reception desk. "Aren't those the flowers she carried in?"

"Dang, whoever those flowers are for she must not like much because that's the ugliest arrangement I've ever seen. First, who gives yellow tansies? I mean, seriously, look at them. They look like a dandelion, which is a weed, and then to mix them with black roses . . . This is a hospital, have some class. Unless you're wishing death upon someone, I think it's best to leave the black roses home," I whisper to Callen as we get closer to the arrangement.

"You sure have strong feelings about flowers, Beswick."

"My mom loved to garden. I picked up a thing or two from her."

He plucks the card from the holder and passes it to me.

My Dearest Steven
Get Well Soon
Your Devoted Mother

"Can I help you with something?" A thin-haired lady appears behind the flowers, poking her head around the large arrangement. Thankfully, it's not the slow fingered nasally woman from last night.

My hand shakes as I work to discreetly put the card back where it belongs. "Um, my dad Steven Beswick. Is he still in the ICU?"

"Let me check," she says, turning to her computer screen.

My mind's racing a mile a minute. Why is Mrs. Jamison delivering flowers for Anna—which, as we know, isn't the real Anna? The real Anna is burning in fire somewhere in another realm.

"Ugly bouquet, isn't it?" she asks, as she catches us eyeing the flowers.

"Hideous," Callen agrees.

The woman's eyes sparkle with joy at Callen's acknowledgement, as if a long-awaited invitation of conversation has been granted. "You know, back in the olden days, people would send their enemies tansies indicating they were ready for war."

A war is coming.

Callen's finger pokes my side, and our eyes meet in a silent wide-eyed exchange. We both know exactly what the other is thinking without saying a word. And this time, it's not our witchy connection.

"Do you know where the lady that delivered these went?" I ask.

"No, sorry, I didn't see her. They just appeared. Sometimes the floral delivery drivers leave them here without a word."

She isn't a delivery driver.

"One time, I came back from my lunch break, and someone had dropped off fifty vases of flowers. I couldn't see over my desk. Can you believe that?"

I politely smile. "So, my dad?" I encourage her to get back to her job.

What's with these receptionists? No wonder things move at a snail's pace around here.

"There's a note on his file. It looks like the doctor tried calling you this morning," she says, looking up from her computer.

"What? No. I didn't have any missed calls." I pull out my phone to check, flashing it at her and then at Callen.

"Sweetie, it also says your father can't have any visitors at this moment."

"No visitors? What does that mean? Is he OK?" I shakily respond.

Callen drapes his arm around my shoulders, pulling me into his side. The warmth of our witchy powers radiates between us, providing me with a sliver of comfort.

"Let me page the doctor," the lady responds.

"Thank you," Callen says, answering for me.

A few moments later, the phone on her desk lights up and rings. She swivels her chair around for some privacy and speaks a little too softly into the receiver for me to hear.

When she spins around, her eyes are cautious. "You can meet the doctor at the nurse's station in the Intensive Care Unit. Do you know where that is?"

I nod.

"But family only." Her eyes fall to Callen.

"I'll be waiting for you," he says, dropping his arm.

"Thanks."

I pivot to rush away, but he pulls me back, wrapping me into his arms, pulling me tightly against his chest. The sound of our heartbeats mingling makes me feel safe, like maybe everything will be OK. I turn to look him in his beautiful dark eyes and press my lips against his warm cheek, kissing him softly.

As I walk away, I can't help but question, why did I do that?

***

"Miss Beswick, nice to see you again," the doctor greets me in front of the nurse's station.

The smell of antiseptic is especially present this morning, along with the echoing sound of machines beeping through the halls.

"How is my dad? Why can't I see him?"

"He had some complications during the night. We have no visitors requested because we can't take any chances of infection. He's stable, but not out of the woods yet."

"His kidneys are doing OK?"

"Like I said, he's not out of the woods yet, but it looks promising. We've been able to flush all the toxins from his body. Now we're hoping his organs continue to fight and return to normal functionality."

"Can I at least stand outside his room for a moment? I need to see him. Please."

He presses his lips into a flat line. "Sure, I suppose that won't hurt anything, but just for a moment, OK?"

I express my gratitude with a warm, sincere grin. "Thank you."

Outside my father's room, I gaze at him through a narrow, rectangular clouded pane of glass. My view of him is distorted, but I can still see all the machines working to keep him alive. He looks so helpless.

I press my hand against the door, trying to feel close to him. "Dad, I love you. The doctor says you'll pull through this if your body keeps fighting. I'll be back later. Don't leave me. Please, Dad, I need you to get better."

My sobs echo in my ear as hot tears wash down my cheeks. I'm about to turn away, but something catches my eye, making me pause for a second glance.

I press my fingertips into my eyes, feeling the wetness of my tears as I try to focus.

It can't be.

It's not possible.

It's Margo's necklace.

CHAPTER 27
TAKE ME TO THE FOREST

The purple and black antique pendant necklace that Margo's always wearing—the same one that showed up last night in Isobel's diary—is laid out on the table next to my dad's hospital bed. With each sliver of movement, the stone seems to pick up a different beam of light, making its glossy sheen glimmer.

I feel sick.

How did it get here?

Is it really Margo's necklace?

The sound of my own ragged breathing fills my ears as I rush to the nurse's station. My heart pounds in my chest like a drum.

"Room B—Steven Beswick—I thought he couldn't have any visitors?" My words come out as choppy as my breath.

"That's right, I'm afraid. No visitors," the nurse responds.

"There's a necklace in the room. How did it get there?" My fingers shake toward his door.

"A woman stopped by and asked if she could leave it. She thought it was good luck and wanted him to have it near him. I thought it was sweet." The nurse smiles.

My body fills to the brim with uncontrollable terror. "Can you please remove it from his room?" My words come out almost hoarse with anger.

The nurse meets my gaze with a piercing glare, like I uttered something terrible. "The woman was adamant that it would bring him good luck, and quite frankly, he needs that. It can't hurt, right?"

"Who was this woman?" I demand.

"She said she was his wife."

Mom?

My stomach lurches.

"What did she look like?"

It can't be my mom.

No.

She's gone.

The nurse squints up at the bright lights, her bushy eyebrows knitted together in concentration. "Long, thick brown hair. Very pretty."

Not my mother.

"That woman isn't his wife. Please, don't let her see my dad, and remove that thing from his room. It's not good luck, I promise you that."

She stares at me with a puzzled expression, but finally gives me a slow, hesitant nod of agreement. "Yes, on my rounds, I'll remove it. What do you want me to do with it?"

"I really don't care."

***

In the elevator, my hands tremble as I anxiously search for my phone.

Where is it?

I swear it was in my pocket, but it's not there. My palms are growing sweaty from my increasing anxiety, and the stuffy elevator isn't helping.

I drop my bag off my back and frantically rummage through it. A sigh of relief escapes me when I finally spot my phone stuffed in the side pocket.

My fingers stick as I attempt to glide over the keyboard. I wipe my hands on my shirt and try again with success.

Izzy: Are you safe?
Izzy: Are you wearing your necklace?

Three green dots flash on the screen.
Hurry. Type faster.

Margo: In class.
Margo: Yes?

It's not Margo's necklace.

Izzy: Take it off now!
Margo: What's going on?

The elevator door glides open with a soft swoosh. I'm immediately engulfed in a loud, hectic atmosphere of coughing patients, sniffling people, and stressed hospital staff.

I hate hospitals.

I slide my phone into my back pocket and hurry into the waiting room, where I spot Callen, his head lolling against the chair.

When he catches sight of me, he stands alert and rushes to my side. "How's your dad?"

"He's doing better. Still not out of the woods, though."

I stare at him, my face heavy with seriousness. "We have a problem."

His eyes flood with worry.

"Mrs. Jamison left another gift. This time pretending to be my mom. You know Margo's necklace? Well, there's one just like it sitting on the table next to my dad. She told the nurse it was a good luck charm. Something's not sitting right. First, she's friends with Isobel, then she's asking about Anna. And now, she's dropping off gifts at the hospital, posing as my family." I pause, reflecting on my words. "Callen, I don't know what's going on, but I need you to take me somewhere."

"Anywhere."

"Take me to the forest. I need to go to Anna's body."

CHAPTER 28
GLAMOUR TRICKS

"I'll take you anywhere you need to go. But why there? Her body's probably not where my parents left it. Anna's been walking around, remember?" Callen says.

"I can't explain it. I need to see the exact place your parents left her. Your mom said it was a quarter mile from the circle and over the cliff. I'm sure we can find it."

"Of course, I'll take you. Izzy, I would do anything for you."

"Why are you so nice to me?" I can't help but ask.

"I told you before. I've never felt a connection with anyone like I have with you. It's like I've known you forever. Plus, I think you're cute." His face lights up with a playful smile, accompanied by a soft chuckle.

"Callen, I don't know what to say." My cheeks flame hot with a mixture of embarrassment and exhilaration.

"So, are we going to talk about that kiss, Beswick?" Callen drapes his arm around my shoulder, pulling me close as he leads us out of the hospital and across the parking lot.

"That was hardly a kiss."

"But it was a kiss."

"It was a sympathetic thank you for being here with me and for being my friend," I respond.

"I don't think hunter boy would like the idea of you going around town offering sympathetic thank you kisses."

"Well, unless we figure out a way to break this curse, it won't really matter, will it?"

I sink into the seat of the car with my face noticeably contorting into a frown. A dizzy array of emotions flash through me as visions of Riley dance through my mind—the hunter side of him and the sweet, sexy boyfriend side of him.

"You know what will cheer you up?" Callen asks, pulling me away from my thoughts.

I shoot him a curious glare.

"A glamour trick."

"Really?" I say, my voice elevated.

"Have you ever thought about what you'd look like with short, black, spunky hair?"

"Can't say that I have, but it sounds like fun."

"Do you have a piece of paper?"

I reach into my bag and tear out a blank piece of paper from my history notebook and hand it to Callen with a pen. He scribbles down some words and passes it back to me.

"OK, so imagine your hair exactly as you wish, while you run your fingers through it, and don't forget to recite this." He points to the sheet of paper.

Callen takes a minute, messing with his phone, then shifts the car into drive and pulls away from the hospital, leaving me to play with my magic as he drives.

I giggle and shift in my seat, eager to finally try something fun and harmless. I weave my fingers through my hair, imagining a completely different style. I picture short, silky, black, punk rock style hair with purple lowlights and fringe bangs as I recite the spell Callen wrote down.

> *"I call upon Venus, Goddess of beauty.*
> *Change me for the world to see.*
> *Find my inner desire*
> *And let it be.*
> *Make me ripe for view,*
> *Only for a fleeting few*
> *So shall it be."*

"I don't think it worked," I say with disappointment.

Callen quickly glances at me, briefly taking his eyes off the road. His face contorts into a funny grin. "Oh, it worked."

"What? Is it bad?" I eagerly yank down the mirror.

"It's just different." He laughs.

I gaze at myself in the small mirror. "It's different, all right." I turn my nose up and frown at my reflection.

"I like the real Izzy better. Please don't decide to go all punk rock on me now," Callen says.

"Don't worry, I won't. So, how do I change it back?"

"Sorry, you're stuck like that until it wears off."

"You asshole," I say, slugging his shoulder. "You should have told me to do something small, like my nail polish."

He winces. "Your tiny little punch is eventually going to leave a mark if you keep hitting me in the same spot. At least try to rotate your physical abuse. And by the way, I'm just messing with you. Shake your head vigorously, while running your fingers through your hair."

I do as he says, and it falls back to my normal dirty blonde color and shoulder length style, with one little purple highlight staying in place. "I think I'm going to keep this one for a little while," I say, stroking the dyed strand of hair.

He chuckles. "Good choice."

"Thanks, I think it's pretty cute."

"Hey, before we get to the forest, I wanted to tell you that while you were talking with the doctor, I found the man you asked about."

"Jonathan Kent. You found him?"

"Yes, and he's very much alive. He's a handyman in West Gate. His picture on his website looks like he's about the right age, and he kind of resembles your dad. I think it's him."

"Callen, that's great news. I have a grandpa. Wow." I shriek with excitement.

Callen pulls his car off the road and parks at the base of the hill by my house. "Easier access to the forest from here," he says, shifting into park. "So, what's your plan?"

"I'll know it when we get there."

CHAPTER 29
I COULD KISS YOU

"Before we start our hike, I have something for you," Callen says, reaching into his trunk.

"You have something for me?"

"Close your eyes and hold your hand out."

I extend my hand, palm facing up, with my eyes tightly shut. He gently places an object in my hand.

"You can open your eyes now."

I gaze at an amethyst in my palm, its facets catching the light from every angle. "It's the one I was looking at in Invoke Awakenings."

"I know. I saw you eyeing it. It seemed like it really spoke to you, and I thought you should have it."

"Oh, Callen, that's so thoughtful of you."

"But fair warning, I did cast a protection spell on it. I know you're not a fan of protection spells right now, but I thought you could keep it in your bedroom, so you'd be safe with hunter boy. I at least have to try, right?"

"It's perfect. Thank you." I slide the beautiful item carefully into the side pocket of my backpack.

Callen reaches back into his trunk and grabs a couple of bottles of water. "It's warm, but it's better than nothing." He passes me one.

"Hey, I think I'm going to shoot the group a text letting them know where we're heading. Just in case something happens, they'll know where we are."

"I already did that," he responds with a smirk.

"When?"

"Does it matter? I have my sneaky ways. They're ditching school, and they're on their way now"—he glances at his phone—"and should be arriving any minute."

"Good. I didn't want to do this without them."

"I figured."

I let my gaze fall to the ground. "Riley too?"

"He was in the group message, so it's up to him if he shows or not. After this morning, it's hard to say what he'll do."

"I could kiss you right now," the words fly off my tongue.

"Haven't you already done that?"

"I meant it like in a figure of speech kind of way."

The sound of tires crunching the gravel causes us both to look down the street. A brand new, sparkling red Jeep pulls up, parking in front of Callen's Cadillac.

I do a quick head count.

I don't see Riley.

A hollow ache of disappointment weighs in my chest, but perhaps it's better this way. He's changing quickly, and most of us are witches. It's not safe.

"Nice ride," I shout to Jessa, who's sliding out of the driver side door.

She confidently tosses her glossy blonde hair over her shoulder as she approaches us, clicking the lock button on the key fob over her shoulder. "I know, right? It's so cute and so me."

"It sure is," I respond.

Seeing the red Jeep gives me a sense of freedom. I no longer have to see the white Jeep—the murder weapon on wheels.

But quickly my attention turns to Margo. My jaw drops when I notice the necklace still hanging across her bare chest.

"I told you to take that off," I snap.

"I didn't want to lose it." She defensively clutches the pendant in her hand. "Sorry, you didn't give me a reason to take it off."

Oh, shoot, that's right.

"Sorry, I got sidetracked with Callen at the hospital. But Margo, trust me when I say it's best if you take it off." I pause, remembering the necklace laid out next to my dad's bed. The image makes my skin crawl. "When I was visiting my dad, the same necklace was in his room. Mrs. Jamison apparently left it for him."

"Our teacher, Mrs. Jamison?" Margo gasps. "She wasn't in class this morning."

I shake my head. "And she dropped off flowers—the card said they were from Anna." I feel sick when I say the words.

Margo undoes the clasp of the necklace, and it slides down her chest and into her hands. She carefully places it inside Callen's open trunk.

"How come everything that comes out of your mouth these days is complicated?" Jessa scoffs.

I frown at her response.

"So, what do you hope to find in the woods?" Tahlia asks.

"I honestly don't know, but I need to go to the place where Anna's body was left. She needs help, and it's the best place to start."

"Are we going to do the séance now?" Jessa asks.

She always wants things to be normal, yet she's the first to jump on board anything witchy. Hasn't this girl learned her lesson yet?

"If we need to," I respond.

"Well, let's get this show on the road," Jessa says, already a few steps ahead of us.

"Margo, are you sure you want to come? I'm not sure how long this will take. I know you have Megan's . . ." I let my words trail off because they don't need to be said.

"It's OK. This is important, and she'd understand. Plus, I'm not sure I even wanted to attend the funeral anyway. I don't want that to be my last memory of her. We'll always have our special place—the pond. I think that's where I want to say goodbye to her."

"I think that's sweet, and I'm sure Megan would've loved that idea."

I wrap my arms around her, bringing her into a tight embrace. "I'm so sorry for your loss. It's not fair. Life's just not fair sometimes," I whisper into her ear, her reddish-brown locks engulfing my face, forcing her sweet vanilla scent into my nose.

Margo's heart beats against my chest, hesitating for a moment before rapidly increasing in tempo. Her body tenses, going statue-like in my arms before shoving me away, her hands cold against my hot skin.

My eyes flutter with confusion.

"Why would you show me that?" Her voice is sharp.

"Show you what?"

"The night Megan died. I saw it. We were all in the car when Jessa hit that animal."

Oh shit. My blocker wasn't up.

Callen's eyes burn with warning as fire sears through me, penetrating deep, making my bones ache.

"I'm sorry. I don't know why I was thinking that."

"Wait. You saw her thoughts?" Tahlia questions.

"Yes, I saw her thoughts clear as day." She glances between Tahlia and me, her expression plagued with tears. "You still feel guilty. Why?"

When I don't respond, Margo reaches for my arm. "Let me see more."

I quickly tumble backward, my body shaking from her aggressive desire to know more. I'm exposed, and she can't see the darkness I'm hiding. It would destroy her. It would obliterate our coven and ruin everything we're working toward. One misstep on my part will unravel the delicate fabric of deceit that Callen and I have woven to keep everything together—to keep our coven safe.

Everyone's eyes narrow on me as I steady myself on the ground below. I study each of them, all with the same expression—confusion.

"What are you hiding, Izzy?" Margo demands.

"I'm not hiding anything."

"Izzy, for some reason, I don't believe you this time." Margo's head drops, and she slowly turns her back to me, walking in the other direction, back toward the street.

"Margo, where are you going?" Tahlia calls out.

"Maybe I'm not up for this little excursion. I'm going to wait in the car."

"Margo, we need you," Tahlia pleads.

Margo sharply pivots, her feet leaving a twisted imprint in the dirt. "Will someone please give me their keys?" Her voice quivers as she holds her shaking hand out.

"I don't want you huffing up my new car," Jessa says.

Are you fucking kidding me right now, Jessa? Give the girl your damn keys.

Callen shakes his head, visibly rolling his eyes at Jessa's bluntness. "Here, take mine." He tosses his keys to Margo.

We all watch as Margo slides into Callen's driver seat, tears streaming down her face.

I can almost feel my heart shattering at the sight of her. This isn't what I wanted.

"She's really not coming back, is she?" Tahlia asks.

"I'm afraid not. She needs some time. It will be OK," Callen responds, squeezing his sister's shoulder, directing her toward our path into the forest.

I pause for a moment, closing my eyes, taking a second to gather the mental strength to continue.

My dad needs me. Anna needs me. I can do this.

"Geez, Izzy, what was that about?" Jessa asks, her voice cutting through my moment of silence. Her timing is always irritatingly impeccable.

"Nothing," I huff.

Just saving your ass.

"Come on, let's go. I don't want Margo waiting too long for us."

When we catch up, Tahlia doesn't look me in the eye. Callen reaches out and squeezes my hand quickly before anyone notices. He knows I'm not to blame. He's the only one that understands right now.

"So, does that mean if we need to do any witchy stuff, I get to be your fourth?" Jessa asks, but no one responds.

Instead, the four of us walk in silence. The only sounds are the crunching branches below our feet and the faint sound of rushing water growing with each step.

When we get to the clearing where we had our circle, it's like we were never here. Callen and Tahlia's parents did a good job of cleansing the area of our presence.

I walk to where Anna breathed her last breath, and the earth hums below me.

"Anna, I'm here." My voice echoes around me as I spin in circles with my arms outstretched, waiting for some sort of guidance. "How can I help you, Anna?" I twirl around, hoping to grasp onto her spirit.

I crumple to the ground, my tears spilling out, obscuring everything into a hazy fog. "Anna, please, I'm here. Talk to me."

"Run, child, run," a desperate, ghostly plea echoes through the air.

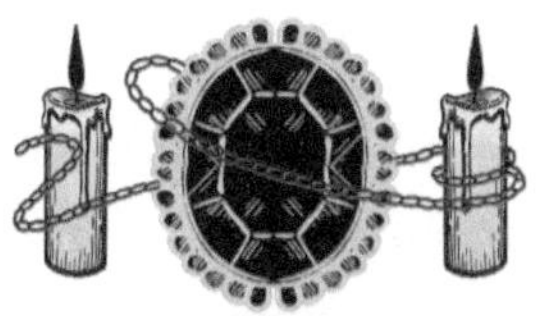

CHAPTER 30
RUN

"Did you hear that?" I cry out.

With a trembling hand, I wipe the tears from my eyes, repeating my words to my friends, "Did you hear Anna?"

No response.

"Hello!" I yell, spinning around, with my watery eyes darting to each corner of our space in the forest.

"Run," the voice cries again, pleading for my attention.

Where are my friends? I can't leave them behind.

A mournful wail vibrates through the air not too far from me, drawing my attention to the tree line.

The tension I didn't realize I'm holding onto releases in my shoulders as I spot the silhouettes of my three friends beckoning me toward them.

"Izzy, someone needs help!" Callen shouts.

The three of them dart into the dense forest, their figures fading into the shadows of the trees.

"Callen, Jessa, Tahlia! No, don't go in there," I scream. My voice seems to reverberate off the trees, my plea going unnoticed as it bounces back to me.

"Run, child. Run away." Anna's voice slices through the dense air, her tone filled with frustration.

With a surge of adrenaline, I take off in a sprint toward the cries for help, ignoring Anna's warning. I'm stalled when I meet the cliff—the one where I assume Anna's body was tossed over just days ago. Standing here, seeing her final resting place, I know there's no way she could have survived if she were alive when Barrett and Bree tossed her over the cliff.

I glance below to see my friends scrambling their way down into the narrow ravine.

"Wait for me," I call out, but they can't hear me over the sounds of the rushing water below.

Carefully, I navigate my way down the rocky embankment, my flip-flops failing me as I slide in and out of them. Loose rocks cut up my bare feet with each movement, slowing me down.

I can hardly make out my friends, who seem to have disappeared in the overgrowth of bushes and plants near the stream. But one thing I can make out is the cries pleading for help, echoing through the forest. I can tell one voice is female, and the other is unmistakably a man's voice.

Perhaps it's two lost hikers needing assistance.

Please be lost hikers.

"Tahlia, Callen, Jessa!" I scream again. I've lost sight of them.

Shit.

I continue upriver. *Callen, if you can hear my thoughts, please be careful. I'm coming. Something's not right.*

The screams for help slowly morph into a chorus of tortured moans, echoing down the stream of water, flooding my eardrums.

My pace quickens until I'm halted by the sight of three people dressed in long, red hooded robes.

What the hell? Not lost hikers.

I stumble back, my breath catching in my throat as I maneuver behind a thick tree trunk, careful not to be seen or heard. The rough bark scratches along my legs as I crouch down. Branches and twigs snap under my flip-flops and I hold my breath, hoping I haven't exposed myself.

Slowly, I allow my head to twist around, letting my gaze slip past the tree.

I squint, struggling to make out their faces, but one thing is crystal clear. Each robed figure is wearing a necklace identical to Margo's.

CHAPTER 31
OTHERS

My eyes are frozen—unable to blink away the sight before me. As I peer through the thicket of trees, the three individuals adorned in red robes are surrounding something on the forest floor, their necklaces swaying with each daunting movement—taunting me.

What am I seeing?

Is this some kind of a cult?

I quickly pan the forest, trying to pick out the hidden faces of my friends. They must be here or nearby, gazing at the same sight, questioning what it has to do with us. But I'm becoming increasingly frustrated as I come up with nothing.

Where the hell are you guys?

Callen, can you hear me?

The tortuous cries tormenting my eardrums have dwindled to a faint whimper, making me more nervous, fearing we might be too late for whatever this is.

I need to get closer.

I slowly inhale, holding my breath, hoping the sound of branches breaking under my feet doesn't give me away. If

I'm caught, I'll be no use to anyone. I pull myself upright and take a cautious step toward the cult.

One slow step at a time, Izzy.

I wince with each crunch, crackle, and snap under my feet.

One of the red robes moves.

Shit. Shit. Did they see me?

The robed person glances around, but then glides to the other side of the group.

They didn't see me.

My heart pounds wildly in my chest.

Now with all their backs to me, I take my opportunity to run until I'm as close as I can get without being right on top of them. I crouch behind a large boulder just in time to hear another visceral cry for help. The group parts, giving only a quick view inside their circle—a witch's circle.

I clap my hands over my mouth—it's Barrett.

CHAPTER 32
ONE TO DIE FOR

No, it can't be—my eyes must be playing tricks on me. I clench my fists, trying to contain the scream that's working its way up my throat.

No, this can't be happening.

But it is.

Even restrained, his posture is impeccable, with his back straight and his shoulders squared. My heart rate flares wildly as a heavy feeling perches in my gut, churning into a swirling vortex of dread. I wish I knew more magic—being a witch is helpful, but being a new witch is frustrating. I want to help him, but I don't know how.

I wildly scan my surroundings. If Tahlia and Callen see this, they're going to lunge at the first opportunity to help their father. I can't let that happen. They'd be walking into the lion's den. But there are no eyes jetting secretively behind the trees as far as I can see. Although, there isn't any way they'd missed this. Their path would have led them right to it, just as mine did.

"Dark Mother, we bring you two offerings," one of the cloaked people shouts, her voice low and husky.

Two? That's right; the woman's voice I heard earlier. Where is she? Dark Mother? What the . . .

Both Barrett and the woman's voice come together in an agonizing cry for help—the woman's voice rising above Barrett's. I gulp, nervously waiting, but expecting to see Bree.

I balance myself on the tips of my toes, feeling the dew on my skin, the morning sun not yet reaching behind my boulder of security. My foot slips, cracking my elbow against the hard, ridged surface. I don't scream from the intense pain, instead I bite my lip and try again.

I scan for the woman, but I can't see her.

The cloaked lady who spoke slowly pulls back her hood. She briefly turns in my direction, revealing her face.

I know this woman, but how?

Think, Izzy, think.

First, the voice and now the face. I've seen her before, but I can't place her.

The rest of the cult slowly backs away, revealing the woman next to Barrett—it's not Bree.

I don't know her. I don't recognize the woman tied up with tears flooding down her pale, round face.

The other two robed ones follow the first woman in removing their hoods, causing me to gasp in shock.

You have to be fucking with me—the tarot lady and the shop clerk from Invoke Awakenings. What the hell.

I knew there was something creepy about that man—the one who eyed Margo's necklace, which happens to be the same one he's fucking wearing right now. And that woman—*there's something attached to your dark shadow.*

You and your cards can go fuck yourself.

I suspect she knew exactly what was behind me, and she might even be to blame. I don't know how or why yet, but I'm going to find out.

The sun streaking in through the dense trees reflects off one of the necklaces and bounces right into my eye as if intentional. I'm sure I'm imagining that, but at the same time, probably not. Everything seems to have a connection, yet I can't figure out what these necklaces are for, and what this all has to do with Barrett and this random woman who are tied up like wild animals.

The first lady calls again, "Dark Mother, are you with us?" Her husky voice shocks a nerve this time.

Oh my God—the bakery lady. That's who she is. The rude lady from East Gate Bakery. She was the cashier the first day I met the girls. Is everyone in this town supernatural, or is this woman just part of some satanic cult?

"We have two bloodline witches as offerings," she continues.

Bloodline witches.

Margo's mom, Mia?

That's the only other person it could be. This isn't good, not good at all. Mia's been hidden—safe. She doesn't practice magic—well, neither does my dad, and he's fighting for his life too.

How can this be happening? What do these people want with us?

"Just a moment," the tarot lady says, walking around Mia and Barrett, both of them crying for help. "We're waiting on our fourth."

Fourth?

"She's attending to some last-minute gifts." The man chuckles.

Mrs. Jamison?

I think I'm going to be sick.

"Show yourselves." The tarot lady dramatically throws her robe open, creating a dominating spectacle. She continues to strut around the circle in a taunting fashion, radiating in her power. "Come out, come out, wherever you are. I know you're here listening. It's time to play."

Busted.

They know we're here. Thankfully, I don't see my friends giving up so easily. They're still hidden like me, but for how long?

"Are we going to do this the hard way? It's your choice. Show yourselves." The tarot lady peers out into the forest, in the opposite direction of me. "Now!" she roars.

The sound of birds scattering from the trees ripples through the air, making the hairs on my arms stand erect. My body turns cold, dropping drastically in temperature, making my skin crawl with goosebumps.

"Your choice," she calls out. "The hard way, it is."

She glides back to her cult and smacks Mia straight across the face. Mia wails in pain, causing more birds to leave their homes, squawking and shouting as they flutter away. Blood drips over Mia's eye and down her face, mixing with the tears.

The three robed ones come together, letting their hands greet one another until they're in a small circle. They start chanting in a language I don't understand. Their words start off soft, then grow louder and faster, seemingly repeating their chant in rounds—they're witches too. Nausea grows inside my stomach, twisting its way up my throat. I swallow hard, careful not to be heard. But the sight that's heading my way causes me to rattle in my stance.

Callen and Tahlia's feet resistively drag against the ground, leaving lines in the dirt as they're pulled into the circle next to the tied-up people.

Where's Jessa? She better be somewhere safe.

"Dad," they both cry, collapsing into him. Their arms fully encompass their father until he's swallowed up by their embrace.

Tahlia breaks away first, twisting her head to the other prisoner. "Mia," she says, reaching to her face, wiping the tears and blood away.

"Well, that was easy. Nothing like a good old force spell to bend a witch's free will," the tarot lady says with a sick chuckle.

"Where's the chosen one?" the man asks. "She should have been summoned as well. She must be here. Where the hell is she? We fucking need her. We can't mess this up."

The chosen one? Are they talking about me?

Suddenly, my body lurches forward, feeling the pull of their spell, but something stops me, tugging me back. The resistance in both directions is so strong I think it's going to split me in two.

All eyes madly scan the forest, searching for my arrival. My coven, wondering if I'm safe, and the cult, wanting to add me to their fucked-up offering.

My body vibrates in an intense zip of energy that whips from my feet to my head, then everything stops. My fire returns, growing hot and fierce inside of me.

Their spell didn't work.

I'm still here.

"She'll come," the tarot lady reassures her group, turning their focus back to my friends.

Oh, I'm coming all right, but not as your prisoner.

"What do you want from us?" Callen demands, his voice stern and powerful. He's taking things into his hands. I can feel it—I can feel him now.

"Tsk, tsk. I can't ruin the surprise," the tarot lady says with a gleeful smile.

"And what surprise is that?" Callen asks.

She lets out a wicked laugh. "Well, you're going to have to wait, now aren't cha? But it's one that's to die for."

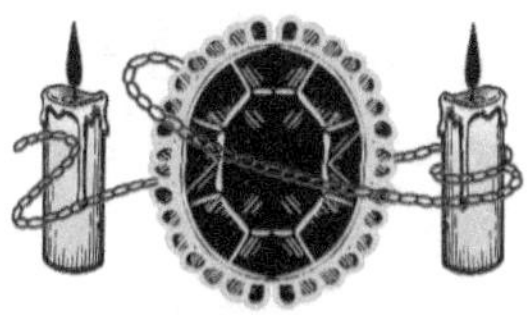

CHAPTER 33
THE HUNTER'S CURSE

I don't like the sound of that one bit. Whatever my plan is, I need to act fast. No one touches my coven mates. I'm their high priestess—the chosen one for a reason. I must protect them at all costs.

I can't hide anymore—I won't.

Taking a deep breath, I mentally prepare to move toward them.

"We may as well get rid of the loose meat; we don't need that one for the fun and games," the tarot lady says.

I pause, freezing in place.

Barrett's cries slice through the air. "No, no. What are you doing? No."

Oh my God. What are they doing?

The robed ones have relocated again, obstructing my view. I try to move, but my feet won't budge—like I'm stuck.

I yank and jerk my feet, but nothing happens. My body is firmly planted in place.

"No," Barrett cries with Tahlia and Callen letting out an excruciating shriek that rattles my bones.

The shop clerk pulls back, and the only view I have is his arm holding an athame with blood dripping down the blade.

"Why did you do that?" Callen cries. "Why did you kill Mia?"

My heart sinks. *Poor Mia—she didn't deserve this.* She had no idea why she was here. Just like my dad—they've done no wrong, and they're paying the greatest price.

Margo, my dear friend. This is going to kill you.

Thank goodness she's not here to see this. My stupid slip of my thoughts earlier might have saved her today.

I can't let another one of our witches become this cult's victim.

I twist and pivot, tugging hard on my feet, but I'm still firmly in place. Seriously, what the hell?

The amethyst—Callen's protection spell. It's working.

Oh, Callen, I could really kiss you this time. You might have saved me and the rest of us by keeping me from their spell.

But you won't like what I'm about to do next.

Sorry, Callen.

I carefully slide the gemstone out of my bag and toss it far away, hoping the thud doesn't gain any attention, and I don't immediately get pulled into their circle.

I take a deep breath, waiting for any movement, but nothing happens. I'm still standing in place, but this time with the free will to move about.

"You're insane," Tahlia screams, drawing my attention back to them.

"You don't get it yet, do you?" the man hisses. "Your bloodlines are tainted, messing everything up for the rest of us. We want freedom from the hunters. The only way to end the hunter's curse is to kill all the bloodline witches. So, you all must die."

Tahlia's mouth parts open, but she's cut off.

"Silence," the bakery lady shouts.

My friends obey.

"See, hunters were never meant to hunt all witches, just the bloodlines who scorned the original Salem witch. But the hunters mutated over time, slowly developing the desire and thirst for all witches of all kinds. Spells don't always turn out as intended, am I right?" He chuckles. "Sometimes magic can be a little finicky. Like the invitation spell. We never meant to include protection for your bloodlines, but that won't matter soon.

"If we kill you all, then the curse ends. The hunters will be freed from their curse, and the rest of the witches in the world will be free to practice as they wish, without fear of being hunted. And now we have one less bloodline witch to worry about." He jovially points to Mia, blood staining the ground around her, seeping into the earth.

"You're sick. You're just as bad as Elizabeth Crowley, wishing ill will on your kind," Callen hisses.

"I take that as a compliment. We worship the Dark Mother herself, and it's our turn to be tested. We're ensuring that your bloodlines won't carry on. We're finishing our Dark Mother's work. And now that the chosen one has arrived, we're free to complete our duty. Centuries of hunters failing is about to end now," the man says with certainty.

I need a plan, and I need one fast. I'm not letting our

bloodlines die at the hands of these greedy monsters. They might be witches, but they're not good. They're worshiping a false god. Elizabeth Crowley isn't a witch to worship.

If Mrs. Jamison is really their fourth, I have a crazy idea that might save us all.

CHAPTER 34
THIS IS WAR

I'm taking a huge gamble assuming Mrs. Jamison is their fourth. I close my eyes and imagine every square inch of her that I can recall from her thick, bouncy, chestnut-colored hair to her thin nose and ruby red lipstick. I picture her wearing a long, red robe over her pencil skirt and white buttoned-up blouse.

I take the spell Callen wrote down out of my pocket, continuing to manifest her image as I recite the words from the paper below.

"I call upon Venus, Goddess of beauty.
Change me for the world to see.
Find my inner desire
And let it be.
Make me ripe for view,
Only for a fleeting few.
So shall it be."

I glance down at my hands, which are longer, thinner, and

aged more than my own. My hair dangles longer, thicker, and brown past my shoulders. Her hideous skirt presses tightly against my thighs. The red robe is heavier than I expected, but it worked.

It's game time.

I summon a deep breath and slowly step forward, revealing myself to the group. I'm cautious with my final steps as I wait for them to see through my ruse. I take another deep breath, preparing to run if necessary.

"Finally," the man huffs.

It's working.

"Where's the body?"

Body?

I don't speak, instead I wait, hoping they'll divulge more.

"I thought Anna's body was with you. Don't tell me you let her roam around again unattended?" he says.

"Norah, I thought you were bringing the other gifts too?" the bakery lady says.

Mrs. Jamison's name is Norah?

"We can't complete our tasks without the others. What's gotten into you today?" the bakery lady asks with disdain in her voice. "And where's your necklace?"

My hand rises to my bare neck.

Oh crap, I forgot to imagine the fucking necklace.

Think quickly.

"I left it with our patient," I respond.

"Yes, you left the one with the window spell, so we could see and hear everything. But you need your necklace to finish our work."

"Margo's necklace?" Tahlia says, looking shocked at her own outburst, her eyes catching on each pendant hanging from their necks.

She didn't notice until now.

The man purses his lips into a flat line. "Margo and Mia's ancestor is a thief. Lydia Bishop stole Elizabeth's necklace. But the joke's been on them because we've been able to see everything. Like we know what you did to Megan Calhoun. Who do you think glamoured that ditzy girl's Jeep the first time? We couldn't have you all in jail when we were so close to breaking the curse."

"Oh my gosh," I cry out, moving my hands to my mouth.

The robed ones collectively turn their gaze my way with questioning eyes.

"She's an impostor. She's not Norah. She's glamoured," the tarot lady says, pointing an accusatory finger at me.

Fear cracks its way down my spine. I open my mouth, my body shaking, the smell of dread filling the forest, and my mission hanging in the balance.

But it's too late.

I've failed.

The sound of rustling branches in the distance pulls everyone's attention away from me. I pivot to run, but I'm pulled back as the real Mrs. Jamison's voice chants in the distance.

"Dark Mother, hear my call.
Change this intruder for all.
Pull her veil from our eyes.
Return her from her way of lies.

> *Dark Mother, I am here.*
> *Protect me and mine,*
> *For it is time.”*

I clench my hands tightly over my ears, trying to block out her words, but it's no use. She has me. I could really use my amethyst right about now.

Her voice reverberates through the air, growing louder as she moves closer, almost gliding toward me. Her eyes lock on mine, and slowly, my body morphs back into myself. I'm no longer the imposter of Mrs. Jamison—Norah—my teacher and the enemy witch. I'm just me—Izzy Beswick—a failure.

"Now, can we finally get on with things?" The bakery lady responds.

"Please tell me you have the body," the man hisses. "I'm ready to end this. These pain in my ass witches—I'm done with them."

"Of course, I do. You fools," Mrs. Jamison responds, pointing to Anna who's emerged from the trees, pushing two people as if she's their guard.

Margo. Riley.

I gag as bile rises in my throat.

"I found these two lingering on the street," my teacher says, making my heart drop.

"Riley, you came," the words slip from my mouth.

He lets his gaze greet mine, but the glint in his blue eyes hardens before he drops his head.

Riley. No. I need you.

Anna forces Margo into the circle.

"No! Margo, don't look," I shout, trying to keep her eyes off her mother's body.

But Margo looks.

The sound of Margo's anguished wail shatters my soul. Her heart-wrenching cries echo through the forest, bouncing off every tree, making us all feel her pain. Each of us wince, wanting to run to her, but it's not possible.

"You monsters. How could you?" Margo hisses to the cloaked ones.

"Cheer up, sweetheart, you're next," Mrs. Jamison says, seething with delight. "But first, one last chance for Elizabeth's hunters to do what was asked of them." She looks to Riley. "It's time to hunt, boy. I know you feel your hate growing for your friends. I want you to kill Margo. Go ahead, get close. Sniff her; smell the witch inside of her."

"Norah, we're losing our body," the man says, pulling her attention away.

Riley doesn't move. Instead, he appears frozen in place with fear etched across his face.

The body of my grandma—Anna—seems to be fading. Her skin is turning nearly translucent.

"Now's your chance to help me, Izzy. Save me to save my son," the real Anna's words slap me hot as if flames were licking my ears, sizzling their way down my neck.

"How?" I mutter.

But there's no response.

The more I hesitate, the hotter my skin burns.

My coven shifts in place, trying to break free from their hold.

"Dark magic," Barrett hisses, twisting his hands in his

ropes. "You brought Anna back to life using dark magic, didn't you?" His words are heavy and drawn out. With each exhale, his nostrils flare, and his breath hums.

"Necromancy is a forbidden magic. I didn't want to imagine that there were other witches out there, especially in East Gate of all places, practicing the dark magics. I spit on all of you. You make me sick."

Heat blazes under my skin. I can't help but think that if this is true, the moment they brought her back to life was the moment I crumbled in my foyer. My connection with Anna shattered briefly, a piece of me dying from our broken connection. That is, until she found her way back to me. Her soul piggybacked on mine, fighting to keep herself pure from their Dark Mother—the dark shadow.

I want to grab the athame from the shop clerk's hand and stab each of them with it.

"Don't get any ideas," Mrs. Jamison says, as if reading my thoughts. She drags me by my wrist, her touch angering my skin. She pushes me into the circle.

"Callen," I whisper, falling into him. I feel a strange sense of calm, despite the looming anticipation of death.

"Dad, can't we do something? A spell to keep us safe," Callen whispers inside our huddle.

"Our spells won't work on dark magic; it's the most powerful form of magic and the scariest. It has no rules, making it very dangerous." He pauses, swallowing hard. "I fear Anna's body, the one in this realm, must be bound to Steven's magic, keeping him ill. If they succeed, then Steven dies, but if we can save Anna first, then your father has a chance," Barrett says.

"Hoods up," Mrs. Jamison shouts. "We must start our offering."

"It looks like our time is running out," I whisper.

The three other rival coven members bow their heads, then flip up their red hoods.

A little dramatic, don't you think?

"Last chance to complete your duty as a hunter. It's time. This is war. Attack Margo. Now!" Mrs. Jamison roars.

Riley nods, and every bone in my body feels like it's breaking, making me crumble to my feet.

"Riley! No," I scream.

He ignores my pleas and predatorily springs toward Margo, coming at her in a sprint.

The rival coven chants.

"Now is the hour of their death.
Now is the hour of their demise.
Now are their final goodbyes."

There isn't anything we can do. My feet are locked to the ground, unable to move. Where are our Earth's gifts when we need them?

"Lock hands. Now," Barrett shouts.

With Barrett still tied up, his children manage to tuck their hands into his. I awkwardly position myself to grab Tahlia and Callen's free hands.

"Stronger with four." Barrett grins.

I feel the vibrations of my coven mates rippling through my body when I catch Riley soaring past us. Riley shoves

Margo in her shoulders, knocking her backward with force.

"Run," he screams.

Riley's quick on his feet as if this were his plan all along. He pivots, skillfully sliding his hand along the robed man's, robbing him of his blood-stained athame.

He flies at Mrs. Jamison in an Olympic sprint, teeth bared and athame forward. He stops just inches from her pretty face, holding the knife still with intent. "I'm not going to hurt my friends, but I will kill you." He presses the knife to her cheek, drawing it down her skin.

A tiny drop of blood crosses down Mrs. Jamison's nose and lingers on the tip before dropping onto her upper lip, mixing with her red lipstick.

When I manage to pull my focus away for the briefest of seconds, careful not to be caught off guard by the others, I'm shocked by the sight—we're surrounded by hunters.

Bree rushes past us at lightning speed, slowing only to wink at us. "Jessa called, filled us in."

Thank you, Jessa. You do have a soul.

Bree dives into the bakery lady, pinning her to the ground. The woman groans as Bree holds her hostage with the threat of her blade.

My nerves rattle as Tim Hawkins comes up on us. My heart thumps rapidly, fearing he's here for me, but he rounds our group and takes the tarot lady by surprise.

"I wanted the bloodline witches dead too, but if that means losing my powers, I'd rather kill you," Tim says, hovering his blade over her chest.

Sid pops out from behind a tree and stealthily grabs the

man, keeping him at bay with a single hand.

Our three heroes trade an understanding glance, then nod in agreement.

"Son, you know what you have to do." Tim's words come out as a low growl before returning his gaze to his victim. Even from my side view of Tim, I know he's enjoying every minute of this. He clenches his jaw, and his eyes turn ice cold. "Riley, now!"

Riley has the knife pressed firmly along our teacher's throat.

The rival coven begins chanting once again in the same language as earlier.

All my cells tingle with an electric current, pulsating the more they chant, forcing our hands apart.

With Callen's fingertips barely staying in my grip, he looks at me and mouths, "Kindred spirits."

Then his hand slips, and we all collapse to the ground.

"Hurry, please," I plead. "They're killing us."

Their chants fill the air, making every bone in my body ache.

Anna's body shakes wildly in the distance, vibrating and glimmering against the shadowed sun.

"Izzy, help," her soul calls out.

Tahlia and Callen scream in agony.

I turn to Tim. "Do it now," I shout, wincing in pain.

He smiles, barreling his knife into the woman's chest— the same way he killed Anna. His smile glistens as he pulls the blade out of the tarot lady's chest.

"My turn," Bree says. She glides her knife across the bakery lady's throat, leaving her blood to rush out her neck toward us like a red river.

Sid, the non-hunter, but loyal familiar, reaches into his pocket and grabs a knife. He stabs the man, and his body falls limply along his side.

"Riley, son, it's time. You must do it. It's in your blood. You were born for this."

The athame shakes in Riley's grip.

"Coward," Mrs. Jamison taunts.

Riley presses the tip of the blade into her throat, pauses, locks eyes with me, then lets the athame slip from his hands. It clatters as it smacks against a rock.

Tim wastes no time, leaping over us with his knife in his hand. Mrs. Jamison has no time to react. Her eyes widen with terror as a blade fiercely enters her chest. A faint whimper escapes from her as she quietly fades in Tim's arms. He turns his lip upward in disgust and lets her body go. The thud echoes off the trees.

All eyes dart to Anna. An intense white light bursts from her body, temporarily blinding us, followed by a sharp crack that strikes through the air, piercing my eardrums, sending a ripple of fire and ice through me. The burning light slowly dims until eventually her body evaporates into nothingness.

"Anna," I cry out.

But the only returning sound is the trees rustling in the wind. I can only assume her soul is safe, and my dad's attachment to that thing is severed.

"Is everyone OK?" Barrett asks.

Soft groans call out from all corners of our area, but everyone seems all right. Although, pain still courses through my body like I've been hit by a truck. I summon what little energy I have left to propel myself upright. Callen's dark eyes call to me, but I ignore him and move cautiously toward my boyfriend.

"Gather the necklaces," Bree orders Sid as I pass them by. "We need to figure out why they're important and how they work."

When I reach Riley, I throw my arms around his neck, but he doesn't wrap me in his embrace like I expected. He stands stiff and erect, keeping his arms pinned tightly at his sides. I feel the tension in his puffed chest.

"Riley?"

He takes a step back, and my hands drop from his body. Tears overwhelm my face, flashing down like a flood.

"No, this can't be it," I cry. "We can still break the curse. Once we figure this mess out. We—"

"You need to get away from me. Now!" he says sternly, cutting me off, his eyes growing darker with each second.

"Izzy, I need you to help me glamour these wounds," Barrett calls out from behind us. "It's all hands on deck right now."

"Coming." I wipe the tears from my soaked face and whisper, "I love you."

Riley's face contorts with conflicted agony, but his body language remains unchanged. "Go," he demands.

"No, Riley," I whimper, remaining firmly planted in place, refusing to leave, willing time to stop. But time has never been on our side.

Riley takes a deep, controlled breath, taking another step back. His eyes smolder into a shadowy, all-consuming darkness, with his lip curling upward.

I'm losing him.

A sharp wave of nausea rushes through my stomach, leaving a sick taste in my mouth. I close my eyes, my shoulders sagging with the weight of my sadness. The faint sound of twigs crunching under Riley's feet makes my heart fall into the pit of my stomach.

I've lost him.

When I gather the courage to open my eyes, Riley's silhouette is already fading into the trees, leaving me utterly gutted and abandoned by the first boy I ever truly loved.

The hunter's curse has claimed him.

I've failed him.

Pain coils itself around all my organs, making it hard to breathe. I slowly pivot, letting my eyes regain focus on my other nightmare; the circle of destruction that encompasses my friends. The putrid scent of death hangs heavy in the air, stirring with each movement of the wind, making my stomach curl. We may have defeated the rival coven and, with good hope, saved my dad, but we are no closer to any of the answers we seek. If anything, we have more questions now.

I need to pull it together and help my coven.

They need me.

I must be strong, but I don't feel strong. I want to crumble into the earth below me. I summon a full breath, allowing my lungs to inflate as I attempt to gather my composure.

I can do this.

Callen's eyes carefully follow me as I walk past him on my way to assist Barrett. His face is weighted with sorrow. I know he wants to run to me, but he doesn't.

I drop to my knees and hover my hands over the bakery lady's throat, just like I saw Barrett do with Anna's wounds.

Focus, Izzy. You got this.

I let my hands rest above her body as I call on my magic.

But there isn't any fire rushing through me; there aren't any vibrations—nothing.

I don't feel my magic.

"You guys, something's not right. I can't feel my magic. It's not working."

"Mine's not either!" Barrett shouts.

"Margo, Callen, Tahlia?" I question.

"No, nothing," they respond in unison.

"The rival coven must have done something to us when they were chanting," Callen says, moving in my direction.

He crouches down next to me and grabs my hands. His dark eyes meet mine, his gaze holding me captive as if he's searching my soul for our connection—our magic—kindred spirits. His eyes swell with tears, making me panic. "Izzy, I can't feel you. I can't hear your thoughts."

Hot tears sting my eyes as I take a shuddering breath and cry out, "Our magic's gone!" My voice cuts through the air like a knife.

"They cursed us—the rival coven cursed us, Callen."

The End.

ACKNOWLEDGMENTS

Writing a series has been such an amazing experience. I love that I get to sit with these characters longer and fully dive into their being. But that comes with a set of challenges, and I'm so grateful that I have such a wonderful community of people surrounding me to help me navigate this new adventure. It truly takes a village to publish a book.

First, I want to thank you, my readers. If you made the switch with me from psychological thrillers, or if you're new around here, I appreciate you! It means so much to me that you chose this book, particularly this series. You're the reason I get to keep doing what I love. Thank you!

As always, I have my husband Jeremy to thank. He's my rock, best friend, and strongest supporter. Thank you for allowing me to pursue my dreams. You're pretty amazing, babe!

To my editor, Nichole Heydenburg, at Poisoned Ink Press. I've enjoyed working with you throughout this series. You've made me a better writer, and for that I can't thank you enough.

To my talented cover designer and illustrator, Natasha MacKenzie. Thank you for creating such stunning artwork. Your work is magic, and it really draws attention. This cover is perfect! I can't wait to see what you come up with for book three.

I can't have my acknowledgments without thanking my amazing family. Dad, for your support and willingness to tell every person you know that I wrote a book. Mom, for your never-ending love and support. Emily, thanks for helping me catch those last typos that slipped through the cracks. Pam for being the final set of eyes before print. Sarah and Rachel, for those much-needed words of encouragement when I feel lost.

To my writing friends who keep me sane, Stacey, Mariëtte, Jessica, Sara, Nichole, Addison, Annemarie, Amanda, and so many more! Your support, ideas, guidance, and advice fuel this writer! I'm so glad we're all on this journey together!

To the Bookstagrammer's I've met over the years, especially @onnikkisbookshelf and @gavinsbooknook. Your support has been amazing.

A special thank you to my ARC and Street Team! You're the best!

Finally, I want to acknowledge my sweet Papillon Daphne, who passed away while I was writing this book. Daphne was my best friend for nearly sixteen years. We had a bond like no other. I was blessed to have had her in my life for so long. She was always by my side while I wrote, making my days so much brighter. Daphne will be greatly missed. Until we meet again, my sweet friend.

ABOUT THE AUTHOR

Jamie Lee Fry is an Oregon-based author with Iowa roots who enjoys creating dark, captivating, and fast-paced stories. When Jamie's not hunched over her desk plotting her next thrilling novel, she's hiking in the mountains with her husband Jeremy and their two dogs. Jamie never says no to a good adventure as long as mountains and waterfalls are involved. Jamie loves documenting life with her camera. She also enjoys stand-up paddleboarding, kayaking, cross-country skiing, baking, and consuming copious amounts of coffee.

CONNECT WITH JAMIE:

@Author_JamieLeeFry

www.authorjamieleefry.com